A NIGHT TO REMEMBER . . .

"So, how're we gonna do this?" Janis said Friday at lunch. "I mean, who's driving?"

"I will," Cassandra said. "What time should I pick you up?"

"Never?" Janis suggested with a grin.

"Don't listen to her," Maria said, laughing. "The dance starts at eight. Brian and I have to be there a little early, so we'll snag a table."

"Oh, I think Simon's coming, too," Janis said suddenly.

"And I talked Gus into nixing the rave," Natalie added.

"OK," Maria said. "That still leaves room for Jesse and Edan."

"What?" Natalie said. "I thought they'd be up on stage, playing."

"They *do* get a break, you know," Maria teased.

"Man, you guys are gonna have so much fun," Stephanie said mournfully. "I wish I could be there to see you win Homecoming Queen, Maria."

"Then why don't you come?" Janis said.

"I can't." Stephanie sighed. "I have to paint the boarder's room. Phillip's gonna help me and I know we'll have fun, but . . ." She shot them a 'what can you do?' smile. "Oh, well, there'll be other dances."

Janis looked away, suddenly ashamed of herself for making a big deal about not wanting to go to this dance. At least she had a choice. She glanced back at Stephanie and her friend's watery, forlorn smile nearly killed her.

GIRL FRIENDS

#2: DO THE RIGHT THING

Nicole Grey

Z·FAVE
KENSINGTON PUBLISHING CORP.

Z*FAVE BOOKS are published by

Kensington Publishing Corp.
475 Park Avenue South
New York, NY 10016

First Printing: September, 1993

Printed in the United States of America

*To Bernie,
for always being The One.*

One

Seventeen year-old Janis Sandifer-Wayne killed the engine of her black Bronco and grabbing her PETA totebag, slid out of the truck. "Rain, rain, go away," she chanted, lifting her face to the gray November sky. Drizzle misted her cheeks, clinging like ocean spray to her straight blond hair and eyelashes. Smiling, she wiped away a droplet forming on the end of her nose. "Not a chance, huh?"

She wasn't really surprised. The slow, constant rain that was as much a part of Chandler's winter as it was nearby Seattle's had held off about as long as possible, and now overcast Saturdays were once again a fact of life.

Hoisting the totebag, Janis ambled up the gravel driveway towards the house. Her father's car was gone but her mother's was in the open garage, tucked amongst the jumbled paraphernalia.

I wonder if those old 'Save the Dolphins' picket signs are still in there, she thought, peering into the shadowy enclosure. We could use the sticks for the anti-fur rally the day after Thanksgiving. Hmm,

I'll have to ask Dad when he gets home.

She took the front porch steps two at a time, the unwieldy totebag thudding against her hip like a cinderblock. The door was unlocked and she stepped into the warm, fragrant house.

"Hi," she called, dropping to her knees as a pair of hysterical dogs barreled into the living room. Laughing, she hugged the shaggy, golden collie/shepherd mix sisters dancing around her like dervishes. "Okay, okay, I'm here! Yes, I love you, too. Where's Mom? Go find Mom."

Luna and Topaz, their soft, liquid eyes gleaming, whirled and galloped away.

"Where else could I ever get a welcome like that?" Janis said, wiping her damp chin on the sleeve of her denim jacket. She reshouldered the totebag, listening to the faint sound of the dogs' toenails *ticking* on the Congoleum and wove through the cluttered room towards the kitchen. Uh oh, she thought, as strains of 'I'd Like to Teach the World to Sing' reached her ears. It was her mother's trouble song, the one she sang whenever the frustrations of Harmony House, the yet-to-be-funded AIDS baby home, were overwhelming and she was convincing herself not to give up.

Janis paused in the doorway, watching as her mother pummeled a batch of bread dough and ground out the song's sweet lyrics. Luna and Topaz flanked her, tongues lolling and wearing triumphant, doggy grins. The housecats, Angel, Isis, and Serene were cuddled on top of the fridge, basking in the oven's rising heat and Star, the young skunk the Sandifer-Waynes had rescued from a steel-jaw trap, was sitting on the counter, patting handprints in a puddle of spilled flour.

"It doesn't sound like you'd like to teach the world to *sing*," Janis said, smiling and slipping out of her jacket. She hung it on the crowded peg near the back door. "It sounds like you'd like to give them all a good kick in the—"

"I thought I heard you come in," her mother said, straightening and flipping her long, blond braid over her shoulder. "Whew. This is the fourth loaf. My aggressions should be gone by now but I think I'm good for at least one more."

"Fine with me," Janis said, dragging her totebag over to the scarred oak table and pulling out a chair. "We eat good when you're crabby."

"I'm not crabby, I'm at my wit's end," Zoe Sandifer-Wayne said, punching the mound of dough on the table in front of her. "What's it going to take to get those babies into Harmony House, Janis? We have everything; the house, the housemothers, a resident nurse, volunteers, toys, furniture, medical supplies and most importantly, those poor little babies . . ."

"But no funding," Janis finished.

"No funding," her mother repeated, giving the dough a mighty whack. "All we need to open those doors is one year's funding and your father and I can't manage to get *anyone* in power to commit. My God, we've done all the renovation and the legwork, how much more sincere could we be?"

"I wish I could do something to help." Janis

brushed a blizzard of flour off the chair and plopped into it. The 'JSW' she'd scratched into the table so long ago protected her seat like a brand. "Hi, guys." She waved to the cats, who yawned, and to Star, who limped across the counter, scrambled clumsily down the series of drawers left open for her convenience and over to Janis. "You've been a good girl?" she asked, scooping her up. She stroked the skunk's silky fur, lingering on what was left of her back leg. The jaws of the trap had mangled it so badly they'd had to have the foot amputated to avoid gangrene but so far Star didn't seem to miss it.

"You *can* do something to help, once Harmony House opens," her mother said. "You can make good on your offer to come down and be Auntie Janis to the kids."

"That's not work, that's the easy part," Janis said, playing with Star's whiskers.

"No, it's not," she said, staring down at the misshapen dough. "The easy part is ignoring the kids, pretending that every HIV-positive baby has a loving home and parents who are willing and able to care for it. The hard part is facing these abandoned children and knowing someday they're going to ask where their families are. Oh, no." She wiped her forearm across her eyes and gave a husky laugh. "Now the bread's not salt-free."

"Mom . . ." Janis didn't know what to say. The kitchen was quiet, as warm and snug as the inside of a mitten, and in this atmosphere it was hard for her to imagine what not having a home or a family

10

would be like. "C'mon, don't cry. You never cry."

"I'm not crying," her mother said, grunting as she heaved the dough into a bowl and covered it with a cotton towel. "The day you see me cry is the day I've given up and I'm not giving up. I'm going to get those babies out of that impersonal, over-crowded hospital or die trying."

"So help you God?" Janis teased, relieved at the militant light in her mother's clear, blue eyes.

"Don't be a wiseacre," she said, lugging the bowl to the pantry and disappearing inside. "Oh," her voice echoed back, "what's happening with Fur-Free Friday, Jan? You never told me. Are any of the friends you made at the Students Against Locker Searches rally into animal rights?"

"I don't know," Janis said, thinking briefly of Brian Kelly, then dismissing the notion as bizarre. He was a major jock who'd risked social suicide to join their student groups' fight against locker searches but that didn't mean he was willing to make a career of it. It was a shame, too, she thought, remembering his chiseled good looks and the sweet smiles he'd sent her way. "We were so busy fighting the locker searches that we didn't have time to talk about anything else."

"And that reminds me," her mother said. "Someone at work gave your father a copy of last week's Chandler News. There's a photo of your student group in there. It looks like it was taken at the rally. He ran off copies and passed them around. He's very proud of you, Janis. Banning locker searches and getting the student body to for-

11

bid guns in school was quite an achievement."

"Thanks. I hope the protest we have scheduled in front of RBK Furriers at the strip mall on the highway goes as well," Janis said, putting Star down and rummaging through her totebag. "It's a new target for the group. I've never been inside the place but I've heard about them. They're supposed to be this very old, dignified, family business and the owner supposedly hates the anti-fur movement with a passion."

"Of course he does," Mrs. Sandifer-Wayne said, coming back into the kitchen. "The fur industry is built on the idea that wearing fur is not only glamorous, but a status symbol. And here you come, showing the world what a fur coat really is."

"Just call us the Myth-Busters," Janis said, setting a stack of anti-fur literature on her lap and paging through it. "Man, you should see some of this stuff, Mom. Documented, filmed proof. For instance; here's a picture of the electrocution rod they use to kill foxes. Guess what part of the fox it's shoved up into?"

"Oh, no" her mother said, looking ill.

"Sure," Janis said grimly. "Hey, can't damage the fur, right?" She cast the evil-looking picture aside and dug further. "And here's a photo of my personal favorite, the steel-jaw trap. See the coyote? See the coyote so terrified he's chewing off his own foot to get away? See the wonderful, 'humane' trapper beating the coyote's head in with the chunk of wood? He's a clever trapper, Mom. He knows that a bullet or a knife would mar the fur and he

12

wouldn't make as much money on it."

Her mother took one look at the photo sequence and turned away. "My God. How could anyone be so cruel?"

"I won't even go into steel-jaw traps and what happens when they catch 'trash' animals," Janis said, gritting her teeth. "But let's just say Star is one 'trash' animal they're never gonna get again." She dropped the literature and scooped up Star. "Never," she vowed into the silky fur. "I don't care who I have to fight."

When the doorbell rang, seventeen-year-old Maria Torres was still up in her bedroom. She hadn't applied her make-up, was only half-dressed, and couldn't decide whether to wear a sweater or a bodysuit with her jeans.

"Maria." Her mother's voice held a smile. "Leif is here."

"Coming," Maria called, glancing at the clock on the wicker nightstand. Her mother, always a sucker for guys with short hair and manners, might think it was gentlemanly of Leif to show up ten minutes early but Maria knew better.

"It just gives him more time to try to get something off of me," she muttered, stopping in front of the mirror. She held up the plum, scoop-necked bodysuit, stretching it around her ample chest and grimaced. The benefit of a bodysuit was obvious; Leif couldn't get into it without some serious maneuvering, but the disadvantage was also obvious;

13

it showed, in great detail, exactly what she was trying to keep him away from.

She flung the bodysuit onto the bed, narrowly missing her cheerleading pom-poms and grabbed the pink angora sweater. Disadvantage; it was easily accessed and even worse, Leif thought she looked like a soft, fluffy kitten in it. "Right, just waiting to be petted," she said, snorting. The sweater didn't seem to have any advantages at all, so she yanked on the bodysuit, topped it with a bulky, cream-colored cardigan, a pair of stretch jeans and plum suede boots. "Ha, try peeling off *this* outfit," she said, grinning at her reflection. Her thick, wavy black hair was tousled and her cheeks flushed with triumph. Her body was *hers* and sooner or later he'd have to understand that.

"Maria," her mother scolded. "You're keeping Leif waiting!"

You wouldn't say that if you knew what he was waiting *for,* Maria thought, tracing her eyes with black pencil. She swished on blush, touched up her lipstick and stuck a pair of gold, triangle earrings through her pierced ears. She stepped back, eyeing her reflection and felt a swift jab of uncertainty. She looked good . . . maybe too good? Was that possible? Leif said so—it was the reason he always gave whenever she got mad at him for trying to go up her shirt—but she'd always thought it was just an excuse.

"Maria!"

"Coming!" She shoved the thought aside and slinging her leather bag over her shoulder, threw open the door. She thundered down the stairs, knowing the unladylike performance would annoy her mother and flashed Leif, who was leaning against the wall, a cool smile. "You're so impatient. If you didn't want to wait, you shouldn't have shown up early."

"Maria," her mother said, frowning at her daughter and giving the hulking linebacker in the varsity jacket an apologetic smile. "Her father and I spoiled her. We never had that problem with her older brother Jesse, but raising a boy is different than raising a girl. Little boys are rough and tumble but little girls should be protected . . . until they become teenagers and decide they can take care of themselves, that is. Then they decide their parents don't know anything—"

"Mom," Maria said, rolling her eyes.

"So spoiled," her mother said, sighing.

"Nah." Leif draped a bulky arm around Maria's shoulders and gave her a squeeze. "She's okay, Mrs. Torres. You just gotta know how to handle her."

Maria stiffened, forcing back the retort that sprang to her lips. One by one, her spiky, red fingernails dug into her thumb, leaving carved, half-moon indentations. On the day I graduate, she thought, catching his smug look, when I don't have to worry about fitting into the jock clique anymore, I am going to poke you right in the eye, Leif. Let Vanessa and Tiffany and all the other cheerleaders say I'm crazy because by then I won't care. And someday Mom, I'm going to tell you exactly what this 'nice boy' Leif kept trying to get off me. See how much you like him then.

"You look lovely," her mother said, brushing a speck of lint from the front of Maria's cardigan.

"Thanks." She shrugged out from under Leif's arm, which lay across the back of her neck like a heavy, wooden yoke. The Seven Pines Badgers football team might celebrate his muscles but she didn't. Brute strength was fine out on the field but when he drank, his octopus-like embrace was nearly impossible to get out of. "Ready?" She plucked her jacket off of the bannister.

"Just say the word," he replied, shoving his hands into his pockets and ambling backwards to the door. "Nice seeing you, Mrs. Torres. Maria's due home by . . . ?"

"Eleven," Maria said.

"Midnight," her mother said at exactly the same time.

Leif's eyebrows rose.

"Well," Maria said, pretending to be pleased. "See that, Leif? My mother trusts you enough to extend my curfew."

"But—" Mrs. Torres began bewilderedly.

"Good *night,* Mom," Maria said, turning her back on Leif and bugging her eyes at her mother. The last thing she needed was for her mother to blab out that the curfew had always been midnight.

Then I'll have to go through a big, wicked scene explaining why I lied about curfew and what am I gonna say? 'See Leif, I kind of liked you at first but then you turned into a lech and now I don't want to see you anymore but Vanessa says only a fool dumps her main squeeze right before Homecoming?' No, she thought, opening the front door, I don't think so. Leif was a bad loser; who knew what his reaction would be if she told him he was wasting his time and that he'd never get any further with her than a few kisses?

So I'm putting up with all his garbage just so I have someone to go to Homecoming with and I don't want to go with him, anyway, she thought, following him down the sidewalk to his Trans-Am and getting in. I'd rather not go at all.

Don't be stupid, a voice in her head that sounded exactly like Vanessa screeched. You're one of the nominees, you *have* to go and you *have* to go *with* someone!

Yes, she did. She'd been tempted to ask Brian Kelly, the popular, currently girl-friendless quarterback if he'd go with her but she hadn't the nerve. What if he said no and Leif heard about it? If she was gonna take that kind of a chance, she at least wanted to be successful. If only Leif would back off a little . . .

She glanced across the shadowy interior. The air was thick with his spicy cologne and a lacy black garter hung like a warning from the rearview mirror. The glowing porch light silhouetted his snub nose and sandy, buzz-cut hair. He revved the engine, leaned over to turn up the radio and caught Maria's gaze.

"What?" he said.

"Nothing," she said, sighing. And it *was* nothing, at least nothing she could put into words. Maybe with someone else, someone who cared enough to know her mind before he jumped her body but not with Leif. This was their tenth time out together and if he'd been the kind of guy she held in her heart, one she hadn't found yet but who she knew would be gentle and kind and caring, she wouldn't have had to wear outfits designed to be body armor or play strategic elbow-games or lie about her curfew. How could she hope to explain that kind of relationship to Leif, when the heaviest thing they'd ever talked about was what color he'd paint the Trans-Am if he ever got enough money?

"Hey." His breath was hot against her cheek. "Remember me?" His mouth found hers, his hand settled on her waist, then began its familiar, creeping ascent.

"We're in my driveway, Leif," she murmured, keeping her eyes closed. If she didn't see the eagerness clouding his gaze and wetting his lips, she could stand it for maybe another minute.

"Maria." His voice was hoarse. "Let's go back to my house. C'mon, just this once." He shifted closer. His hand inched higher. "C'mon."

I should've made plans for tonight, she thought, locking her elbow at her side and trapping his hand against her lower rib. I should've called one of the girls from the Students Against Locker Searches rally. I bet Janis Sandifer-Wayne doesn't have to stay with a guy just because everybody wants her to. And that Natalie Bell, I bet she doesn't do *anything* anybody wants her to —

18

"Maria?"

"No," she said, pulling back and resisting the urge to wipe her mouth on her sleeve. He was watching her, his face close. She forced a smile. "You said we were going for pizza and I'm *hungry.*"

Her words hung in the silence.

"So am I," he said in an odd voice and shifting the Trans-Am into reverse, roared out of her driveway.

I'm gonna ask Brian to the dance, she decided. What's the worse thing Leif can do? Break up with me? Boy, I hope so.

Two

"I can't believe this town is so dead on a Saturday night," sixteen-year-old Natalie Bell grumbled, staring out the BMW's passenger window. "Chandler sure isn't anything like L. A."

"It sure isn't," her seventeen-year-old cousin Cassandra Taylor agreed wryly. "No muggings, no carjackings, no rapes, murders, or riots. Wow, what a shame."

Natalie shot her an irritated look and shifting, tossed her beaded, mahogany-brown braids back over her shoulders. "Don't be mocking me, girl. You know what I mean. It's Saturday night, where's everybody hanging?"

"How should I know?" Cassandra said, braking for a red light. "I'm usually practicing ballet all night. Which I would be doing now if you hadn't coerced me into 'cruising' with you," she added pointedly. The light turned green and she accelerated, heading for the end of Main Street. "Natalie, we've been out here for two hours. Why don't we just call it quits and go home?"

"I don't want to go home," Natalie said, thrusting out her chin and tugging her 'X' cap down over her eyes. "There's nothing to do there."

"You could read your letter," Cassandra suggested.

Natalie folded her arms across her chest and stared out the window. No I can't, she thought, pretending to watch the scenery slip by. If I read my mother's letter, it's gonna say things like 'I miss you' and 'Why haven't you called or written?' and I'm gonna have to come up with some kind of answer and forget *that*. She knows she sent me out of South Central L. A. so I would get a decent education and live to graduate high school, and she knows how I feel about her and her . . . her . . .

Whiteness? her conscience said. Come on Natalie, you floated between worlds for sixteen years and you've finally picked your side — African-American — so why should the fact that your mother's white bother you? Because you look in the mirror and instead of seeing your cousin Cassandra's dark skin and delicate, regal beauty, you see your mother's sturdy curves and light, greenish eyes staring back? Or is it more than that? Is it because your mother's an L. A. cop and you couldn't stand to even look at her after the riots? Is that why you started hanging on the street with people she told you to stay away from? Is that why you challenged everything she said, until there was nothing but screaming arguments and cold, stony silences?

Shut up, Natalie told herself. I don't want to deal with this now. It's Saturday night and I want to have some fun.

"Natalie?" Cassandra's touch was feather-light. "I'm sorry, I didn't mean to bring up a bad subject. We can cruise a while longer if you'd like."

Natalie's bad mood faded as quickly as it had arrived. "Tell you what," she said, swiveling in the seat and giving her cousin an enthusiastic grin. "Forget Main Street. Let's head out onto the highway towards Seattle."

"Seattle?" Cassandra's well-modulated voice rose. "I'm not driving up to Seattle! My parents would have a fit if they found out we left Chandler without telling them."

"How are they gonna find out, Cass?" Natalie said teasingly. "I won't tell and there's nobody else here. Unless maybe you talk in your sleep . . . ?"

Cassandra's knuckles tightened around the steering wheel. "I don't talk in my sleep, don't call me 'Cass,' and we're not going to Seattle."

"Okay, fine," Natalie said, slumping and pretending to pout. She really hadn't expected to go all the way to Seattle which, with the traffic so light, would have only taken maybe twenty minutes anyway, but through experience she'd found that if she asked for *more,* once the bargaining was done she usually ended up with exactly what she'd originally wanted. "Then can we just cruise the highway for a while? I'm so sick of Chandler."

"And . . . ?" Cassandra said expectantly.

"And what?"

"Natalie, you've been with us for over a month. I know there's more than boredom lurking in that

22

pointy skull of yours."

"My skull isn't pointy," Natalie said, trying to throw her off the track.

"Don't change the subject." Cassandra slowed for another light. "The highway's up ahead. Tell me your ulterior motive or I'm turning around and going straight home."

"Man," Natalie said. "Uncle Marlin was right; when a Taylor sets her mind on something, it's as good as done."

"Leave my father out of this," Cassandra said, easing forward as the light changed. "One more block . . ."

"Oh, all right," Natalie said. "Gus from school says a bunch of people rented a warehouse and are throwing a rave tonight."

"What's a rave?" Cassandra said. "And talk fast, we're almost to the entrance ramp."

Natalie shot her an incredulous look. "You've lived here all your life and you don't know what a rave is? Okay, okay, it's a big all-night party with a DJ and stuff. Get on the highway."

"Were we invited?" Cassandra asked, pulling over before the ramp to let the people behind her pass.

"*Nobody's* invited, everybody just shows up," Natalie said, bouncing in the seat. "Now come on, get on the highway!"

"But—"

"Pleeeease get on the highway," Natalie wailed, grabbing hold of Cassandra's taupe, suede jacket. "Look, we have nothing better to do. If it's bad

23

we'll leave but can we just go up there already? Take a chance for once in your life!"

"Don't call me Cass," Cassandra said, scowling and flooring the BMW. They shot onto the ramp and merged with the traffic.

"Thank you," Natalie said, grinning and easing back in the seat. This was going better than expected; they were headed to a major do, the radio station she'd coaxed Cassandra into leaving on was playing Neneh Cherry's 'Buffalo Stance,' and her feet, which hadn't danced in so long, were picking up the old rhythm.

Cassandra glanced over at Natalie. "How far up is it?"

"Uh . . . I'll let you know," she said, sitting up straight.

"Well, make sure it's before I have to turn in. I don't want to get into an accident — "

"We won't," Natalie said, watching the buildings whip by. A hotel, bar and bowling alley. A trucking company. Two abandoned buildings. An open field. I guess I should've asked Gus exactly where it was gonna be, she thought guiltily. And I probably should have made sure it was definitely happening tonight. I *think* he said tonight . . . or did he say next Saturday, the same night as Homecoming?

"There's a warehouse," Cassandra said, signaling. "Right up there, between that bar and the Dunkin' Donuts. But the parking lot's empty and it doesn't look like anybody's there. Maybe they didn't start yet?"

"No, it's almost ten, it would have started by

now," Natalie said, sighing. "I bet it *is* next Saturday night."

"*What?*" Cassandra said, turning into the warehouse's vacant parking lot and screeching to a halt. She put the BMW in 'Park' and taking a deep breath, leaned back in her seat. With calm, precise motions she smoothed her neat, black hair, adjusted her lavender sweater and when the silence had stretched to epic proportions, looked over at Natalie.

"Er . . . I just remembered Gus said something about how the rave was supposed to be the same night as Homecoming," Natalie said, squirming. "Sorry, Cass . . . I mean, Cassandra. I really did forget."

"So it isn't tonight?" Her dark eyes were twinkling. "Oh, that's a shame. I guess we'll have to go home now."

"I guess," Natalie said reluctantly. "Man, this must be your lucky night." She folded her arms across her chest and grumbled, "If I had a car and a license, I wouldn't *ever* go home. I would cruise all over—"

"Look," Cassandra said suddenly, braking before she pulled onto the highway. "Isn't that Maria Torres's brother's band?"

Natalie's head snapped up. "What? Where?"

"Right there," Cassandra said.

Natalie followed her gaze to a shabby plastic sign posted in front of the building next door and her heart began to pound. 'Saturday night,' the sign read. 'Corrupting Cleo.'

25

"It was nice of them to play at the rally last week," Cassandra said, peering over her shoulder to gauge the approaching traffic. "And if they're as big as everyone says, then it's even nicer that they're willing to come back to Seven Pines High and play the Homecoming dance, too."

"Yeah," Natalie said hoarsely. Corrupting Cleo was here, now, playing the dive right in front of them. She opened the window and stuck out her head, letting the drizzle cool her flushed cheeks. She couldn't hear any music, only the whoosh of passing cars; did that mean the band hadn't gone on yet? Did that mean that Edan Parrish, the tall, rangy lead guitarist with the fawn-colored eyes and rippling, honey-blond hair was inside, leaning against the bar or over the pool table, talking and laughing with a crowd of groupies?

Better them than me, she thought, shivering as she remembered his warm, lazy smile. Everything about him spelled trouble, from the fact that he was a white musician to the way his faded jeans hugged his legs, looking as soft and smooth as baby's skin. Except for the hole ripped high on his thigh, she thought, swallowing hard. The one showing tanned skin and golden leg hair—

Stop it, she told herself firmly. Just because he dedicated a song to you at the rally doesn't mean he likes you . . . and even if he does, it doesn't mean you're going to like him *back*. He's bad for you, worse than any of your old, cheating L. A. boyfriends. He's a heartbreaker and your heart doesn't need to be broken again. You swore off guys, especially slick white ones and you're gonna stick to it.

"If they *are* that big a band, I wonder why they're playing a dump like . . ." Cassandra scrunched down to read the sign, "Iron Mike's?"

"Let's find out," Natalie heard herself say.

"But it's a bar," Cassandra said, wide-eyed. "How are we going to get in without ID?"

"Leave that to me." Natalie's heart was thundering and her blood racing but she felt removed, like she was watching some other stupid, starry-eyed girl jump into the volcano. "You just pull into Iron Mike's."

"But I don't want to drink," Cassandra said, getting upset.

"We're not gonna drink. I'm not *that* stupid," Natalie said. Her skin was tingling and she felt like jumping out of the car and sprinting for the door. What was Edan doing while they were sitting here arguing? "C'mon, Cassandra. Go."

"I know I'm going to be sorry for this," Cassandra muttered, driving around the downed telephone poles separating Iron Mike's parking lot from the warehouse's. "What if we get arrested?"

"For what? Playing pool? It says right on the sign that they have pool tables," Natalie said, sounding much more confident than she felt. Sure, she'd hung out at plenty of clubs back in South Central L. A., flashing fake IDs or just sauntering in with an older group, but those had been neighborhood joints filled with people she'd known. She'd never walked into a place blind before, armed with nothing but one bizarrely innocent cousin and a tide of yearning stronger than caution.

"Do you really think we should?" Cassandra asked, staring at the gray, barracks-like building. "I mean, this could be a bad place. What if they don't . . . um, like us?"

"You mean what if it's a skinhead bar?" Natalie said baldly, watching the shocked expression cross her cousin's face. "Tell you what; *if* we can even get in, we'll hang by the door and check the scene for a while. If you hear anyone make any type of comment, especially a racial one, you tell me and we're outta there. Fair enough?"

"I guess." Cassandra sounded unconvinced.

"Look," Natalie said, pointing. "That group of girls is going inside and they look normal enough. All white but not neo-Nazi-ish. Come on, Cass. Let's do it."

"Don't call me Cass," Cassandra said, taking a deep breath and opening her car door. "I can't believe I'm doing this."

Neither can I, Natalie thought. She shouldered her purse and chin high, strode towards the entrance.

The sagging, wooden door opened to a short, shadowy hallway. A guy on a stool blocked the end of the passage and beyond him people of all ages, colors, and clothing were clustered at tables in front of a brightly lit stage. The air was heavy with perfume, french fries, and cigarettes and off in the distance, the *thunk* of pocketed pool balls could be heard.

"Let me do the talking," Natalie said, tugging her cousin inside. "You just stand there and look totally bored."

"Why?" Cassandra whispered.

"Because that guy's gonna card us. Try to look like you're twenty-one and you think it's funny that he wants you to prove it." Straightening her shoulders, Natalie strolled up to the bouncer on the stool. "How you doing?" she said, continuing past.

"ID," he said, holding out a hand and blocking her.

Natalie laughed and glanced at Cassandra, who raised an eyebrow. "When I'm forty I guess I'll enjoy this but now it's just insulting."

"Yeah, sure." His hand never wavered. "ID."

Frowning, Natalie stared past him into the room. The band's equipment was up on stage and seeing Edan's guitar case propped against an amp made it seem very important to get in. "I don't have a driver's license," she said, mixing this truth with a white lie. "I lost it for driving drunk." She heard Cassandra gasp and prayed her cousin didn't look as shocked as she'd sounded.

"That's what they all say," he said. "No ID, no inside."

Natalie lifted her chin. "Look, this is getting old." She paused, crossing her fingers and said, "Edan Parrish from Corrupting Cleo should have left our names at the door. Why don't you see if we're on the list?"

"We don't have a list," the guy said.

29

"Oh, for . . ." Natalie heaved an impatient sigh. "Okay, let's try this. You wanna send somebody back to tell Edan that Natalie Bell is here?" She planted a hand on her waist and assumed her attitude stance. "Or I'll be glad to go tell him myself—"

"Keep your shirt on," he said, waving over a waitress. "Do me a favor. Go back and tell Edan that . . ." He looked at Natalie.

"Natalie Bell," she said.

"Natalie Bell is out here. She says he was supposed to leave her name at the door." He and the waitress exchanged knowing smirks before she left.

"What was *that* all about?" Natalie said testily. She knew what the look had meant—he thought she and Cassandra were a couple of groupies here to throw themselves at the band—but she wanted to make him say so, she wanted to embarrass him the way the smirk had embarrassed her. He'd made her feel stupid and cheap and if it hadn't looked like they were surrendering, she would have marched Cassandra right out of there.

The bouncer shrugged and leaned back against the wall.

"We'll be humiliated if Edan doesn't remember your name," Cassandra whispered, knotting her fingers together. "Maybe you should've said you were his sister or something."

Natalie shot her an incredulous look. "Oh, right, there's such a family resemblance. Edan's white, remember?"

"So, you're light and half-white. You could've

30

passed as his sister."

The thought agitated her. "Stop talking stupid. First of all he might have a real sister and even if he doesn't, I sure don't want to be his sister—" She broke off, scowling as Cassandra's boot crashed into her shin. "Ow, what the—"

"Hey, Natalie, Cassandra. Glad you could make it."

The deep, satin-smooth voice nearly sent her to her knees. I should never have come, she thought, gazing up into Edan's gleaming, amber eyes. "Hi."

"Boy, are we glad to see you," Cassandra said and gasped as Natalie's elbow burrowed into her side. "Ow. Well, we *are*."

"Don't tell him that," Natalie whispered furiously. "He's conceited enough already." She caught his amused look and clamped her lips shut.

"Hey Edan, you know these two?" the bouncer said.

"Sure," Edan said, giving Natalie a devilish look. "We're old friends. C'mon Nat, we have a table up front." His strong, calloused fingers closed around her arm, drawing her past the bouncer and into the main room. "Sorry I 'forgot' to leave your name at the door but I didn't know you were coming," he said with a mischievous grin.

"Neither did we," Cassandra said. She had a hold of Natalie's other arm and was sticking to her like a barnacle. "Natalie thought there was a rave out here tonight but when we pulled in, the warehouse was empty."

"The rave's next week," Edan said, steering the

31

girls towards an empty table with a 'reserved' card on it. "The same night we're playing your Home-coming dance."

"I know," Natalie said, finding her voice. Since when had she been willing to let a guy lead her around, especially a guitar player with a thousand groupies, a lazy smile and a butt too cute for his own good? Since never, she thought, rejoicing as the familiar, prickly cactus feeling flooded her veins. She stepped back, forcing Edan to drop his hand and lifted her chin. "I'm looking forward to it." She waited until his lips curved into a confident smile, then said, "I've never been to a rave up here in Chandler before."

He stepped back, surprised. "But it's the same night as your Homecoming dance. And we're play-ing it."

She arched an eyebrow. "Right . . . ?"

Their gazes locked for a long, charged moment.

"Come to the dance," he said, reaching out and tugging gently on her hair. "Please?"

"I didn't say you could touch me," she said as his knuckles grazed her cheek. Her skin tingled and she was sweating; was that her own breath she could hear, rasping in her throat?

"Then I won't do it again until you say it's okay," he said with a wicked smile. "How does that sound?"

It sounds like I'm in way too deep, Natalie thought, half admiring his nerve. "Cocky," she said instead, meeting his smile with a challenging one of her own. She might be in too deep but she'd rather die than go down without a fight. "And exactly what I expected."

Edan laughed. "You're a real wise guy, aren't you, tiger?"

"Think what you want," Natalie said with a shrug. "It'll be wrong no matter what."

He tilted his head, his wavy hair raining down like a golden waterfall. "Want to make a bet?"

"No," she said, enjoying herself. "You have nothing I want."

His eyes went smoky. "Care to bet on *that?*"

Oh, no, you don't, she thought. It's not gonna be that easy. "Well . . ." She planted a hand on her hip and stepping back, started to give him a very slow, thorough once-over.

"Natalie!" Cassandra blurted, looking horrified.

"What?" Natalie said, tearing her gaze, which had grown way too fond of the perusal, away from his lean, muscled stomach. She looked up, meeting Edan's eyes and a bolt of hot, invisible lightning passed between them.

"Hey, Edan five minutes," someone called.

"Thanks," he said, but didn't look away. "Are you guys gonna stick around for the whole show?"

"Uh . . . I don't think so," Cassandra said, glancing at her slim, gold watch. "We have—"

"Other places to go," Natalie finished, before Cassandra could say 'a curfew.'

"At least stay until our first break," he coaxed.

"Edan!" someone shouted. "Come on!"

"Natalie?" His gaze held hers.

"We'll hang for a while," she heard herself say

and at his triumphant smile, added darkly, "but don't get your hopes up."

"Too late," he said, laughing and sauntering away.

But it wasn't for her. Not this time. A surge of adrenaline flavored with panic shot through her, double-timing her heart and flooding her veins with ice. If she stayed here any longer she would be lost. "C'mon Cassandra," she said, wheeling and grabbing her cousin's arm. "Let's go."

"But we just got here," Cassandra sputtered, gaping at her. "And you just told Edan we'd hang around—"

"Well, I lied," Natalie snapped.

"But . . . but . . . shouldn't we at least tell him we're leaving?"

"No!" Seeing him again would be the *worst* thing she could do. She would look into those smoky, amber eyes and all the good sense she was born with, all the rotten, hurtful love lessons she'd learned the hard way would fly right out the window. She would forget, like she just had, all the times she'd been cheated on by first white, then black guys and how her last boyfriend had said he'd loved her and then gotten her best friend pregnant. She would forget the way her heart had ached and how lonely she'd been, wondering why no one could love her enough to stay—

"Natalie?" Cassandra said.

"We're outta here," Natalie said hoarsely and they left without a backwards glance.

Three

Sixteen-year-old Stephanie Ling stood on the frost-heaved curb between her mother and her little sister Corinne, watching the moving van rumble away. The truck backfired and the explosion echoed through the sleepy, Sunday morning silence.

"Goodbye Alma," Mrs. Ling called, waving as the woman in the Toyota followed the van down the road. "Good luck in your new condo!"

"Good riddance," Stephanie said under her breath. "I hope your ceilings leak and your super's a lazy bum, Alma."

Corinne giggled. "You're funny, Stephie."

Stephanie grinned and stroked Corinne's soft, black hair. "Too bad Mom doesn't think so, huh?"

Mrs. Ling wrung her hands. "Alma wasn't a bad boarder. She made things easier for me—"

"And harder for me," Stephanie said and mimicking Alma, whined, " 'Stephanie, my window latch needs oiling. Stephanie, the door hinge squeaks. Stephanie—' "

"—and the parents of the children I babysit were reassured to have two adult women in the house—"

"One woman and one Medusa," Stephanie muttered, flicking her long, black hair back over her slim shoulders. She'd pay for this rebellion later in ways she hated to think about, but for now the relief of having Alma gone was too good to squelch. Sure, now that their only boarder was gone they would have even less money but Stephanie had already asked Jen down at The Green Café if she could put in extra hours working the cash register and Jen had agreed. "I, for one, am glad she's gone."

"Me, too," Corinne said. "I hated when she told the mailman she was afraid to get a puppy because we were Chinese and everybody knows Chinese people eat dogs."

"Get out," Stephanie said, staring at her. "Did she really?"

Corinne's head bobbed emphatically. "I told her we were Americans of Chinese descent but she didn't care."

"The old bat," Stephanie said.

"—and sometimes she would run to the grocery store when I was busy," Mrs. Ling said fretfully, oblivious to the fact that no one was listening. "I don't know what I'm going to do now that she's left us. You girls will just have to pitch in more."

Here it comes, Stephanie thought, stifling a sigh. Sure Mom, whatever you say. It's not enough that I'm pulling straight A's in advanced classes, working almost full time and doing most of the housework, now you're going to attack the little bit of free time I have with—

"You'll have to spend less time with Phillip, Stephanie. I never liked your riding around on that motorcycle with him, anyway. I'm sure my babysitting clients think he's in a gang. One of the mothers saw you two last week and she's been cold to me ever since. Less time with Phillip. That's the only way."

Stephanie looked away. "We'll see."

"And Alma's old room has to be cleaned—"

"And spackled and painted," Stephanie said, steering the conversation away from her boyfriend. "Alma left crater-sized nail holes in the walls. Don't worry about the cost," she said, catching her mother's wince. "We'll take it out of her security."

Her mother looked away.

Stephanie's stomach sank. "We *do* still have her security, don't we?"

"She made such a fuss . . ." Mrs. Ling's hands fluttered, smoothing her housedress, her hair, her arms. "I gave it back."

"Not the whole thing? Mom, how could you?"

"I asked you to handle it but you said you were too busy," Mrs. Ling said defensively. "And she's such a *determined* woman."

Stephanie didn't hear the rest. She was watching Anastasia, her younger sister trudging down the porch steps. Is that lipstick she's wearing? Stephanie wondered, narrowing her black, almond-shaped eyes. And if that square bulge in her jacket pocket wasn't a pack of cigarettes, she'd paint Alma's whole room with a toothbrush.

"Later, guys," Anastasia said, flipping a nonchalant wave and heading out across the sparse lawn.

"Where are you going?" Mrs. Ling called.

"Out," Anastasia said without stopping.

"Oh. Well, have a nice time," Mrs. Ling said. "Stephanie, do you really think she should go out wearing lipstick? I mean, she *is* only thirteen years old . . ."

"Hold up, Ana," Stephanie called, motioning her sister back. "What's with the lipstick?"

"What lipstick?" her sister said, smirking.

"Oh . . . maybe she isn't wearing any," Mrs. Ling said nervously.

"If she isn't, then she's dead," Stephanie said with a snort. "Nobody's lips are that shade of purple."

"Shut up," Ana said, flushing. "You don't know everything."

"I know a pack of cigarettes when I see one," she said, reaching over and deftly plucking the pack of Newports from her sister's pocket. "What's this?"

"Nothing," Anastasia snapped, grabbing them back. "I'm just holding them for someone, okay?"

Mrs. Ling looked up at Stephanie. "Well, if she's just *holding* them . . ."

"Fine," Stephanie said, feeling the same old sense of frustration she always got when she was dealing with her mother. It had been seven years since her father had left and her mother hadn't coped with one problem since. "I'm going in. Phillip should be here soon and he'll take me straight to work later."

"But what about Alma's room?" Mrs. Ling said, wringing her hands. "The sooner it's cleaned, the sooner we can advertise for another boarder."

Stephanie turned, watching Anastasia walk away.

"I'll take a look at it after work," she said, surrendering.

Maria stood staring into the refrigerator, wondering why there was never anything good to eat, when she heard a key in the front door. Curious, she shut the fridge and tightened the sash on her burgundy bathrobe. Her parents weren't due home from church for another forty minutes and the only other person with a key was—

"Anybody home?" her brother Jesse called from the foyer.

"No," Maria said, grinning.

"Very funny, *mija,*" he said. "Come on in, Edan. Maria's the only one here and if we ignore her, maybe she'll go away."

"And let you two eat us out of house and home?" she said, padding across the kitchen to the coffee maker. "Not a chance." She measured out the ingredients, smiling as her older brother strolled in and tossed his ragged, denim jacket across a family room couch. "I'm making coffee."

"Great. Mom and Dad at church?" he asked, smoothing back his long, glossy-black windblown hair and plopping down in a chair at the table.

"So, what else's on the menu, *mija?*"

"Plenty, if you guys are cooking," she said, smirking at Edan. "If not, then coffee's as good as it gets. Hi, Edan. How're the groupies treating you these days? Still lining up to become your love slaves or what?"

"None of your business," he said with a good-natured grin. "You know Jess, ever since you moved out I'd forgotten how charming your kid sister is in the morning. What does she do, gargle with battery acid?"

"Nah, she's only mean to us," Jesse said, flipping open the Sunday paper and pulling out the funnies. "The rest of the time she's playing Miss Congeniality to her Nordic Neanderthal."

"Don't call Leif names," Maria said half-heartedly, because after last night she was tempted to call him a few herself. The bodysuit had stalled but not stopped him and his hand had gotten a lot higher than she'd wanted. His grope had been fast, sweaty, and outside her clothes but she felt like it had left a slimy, glistening trail from her waist to her breast like a banana slug sliding across a sidewalk.

"You're still seeing that bozo?" Edan asked, slipping into a chair. "I figured since he wasn't at your SALS rally you guys had broken up."

"No such luck," Maria said, retrieving three mugs from the cabinet. "He went to a party at Vanessa's house after the game. It's sort of a tradition that the cheerleaders throw a minor bash whenever we win a game."

"Sure, why go to a rally to defend your rights when you can go to a kegger and get blasted?" Jesse said, shaking his head. "Hey, those jocks know the true meaning of life."

"Like you guys are such angels," Maria scoffed, pouring the rich, fragrant brew. She wasn't sure why she was defending Leif; maybe because admitting he was an idiot would be a reflection on her taste in guys.

"I'm an angel," Edan said, raising his hand.

"Right," Maria said, carrying the mugs to the table. "And I'm marrying Axl Rose tomorrow."

"Outstanding," Jesse said, looking up from 'Calvin and Hobbes.' "Maybe Corrupting Cleo can open their next concert."

"I am," Edan said, leaning backwards in his chair and swiping the sugarbowl from the counter.

"He's in love," Jesse said, rolling his eyes.

"Shut up, Torres," Edan said, scowling.

"Really?" Maria set the cream on the table and stared at him with renewed interest. Edan had hung around with Jesse for so long that she didn't even really see him as a person anymore, he was just another teasing, pain-in-the-butt brother she had to deal with. But Edan in love . . . well, that could be educational. Jesse said he'd never been in love and Maria *knew* she'd never been in love, so if she picked Edan's brain, maybe she'd find out how to recognize love if it ever came along. "What does it feel like?"

Edan avoided her eyes. "Can I have a spoon, Maria?"

"Only if you tell me what it feels like," she said, grinning and blocking the silverware drawer. "C'mon, spill your guts. Who is she? Does she love you, too? How do you know?"

"Help me out here, Jess," Edan said, nudging him.

Jesse shrugged and turned the page.

"Uh . . . hey, two of your rally buddies showed up at Iron Mike's last night," Edan said, tugging at the neck of his t-shirt. "Natalie and Cassandra? You remember them?"

"Of course I remember them," she said, studying him. This was definitely not the cool, easy-going Edan she'd always known. How intriguing. "And don't try to change the subject. We were talking about your true love, here."

"Geez, Jess, can't you do something about her?" Edan asked, shifting uncomfortably.

"I told my parents to pinch her off at the neck at birth but —" Jesse laughed, pretending to cower as Maria shook her fist. "Lay off, will you *mija?* The poor guy's striking out big time —"

"Jesse," Edan ground out.

"Oh," Maria said, with a rush of sympathy. She opened the silverware drawer and took out a spoon. "Here, Edan. I'm sorry. I didn't know she doesn't love you back."

"Oh, God." Edan dropped his head into his hands, his thick hair streaming down around him like a curtain and muttered a few choice curses. "Look, forget it, okay? Just because I'm not cattin' around doesn't mean I'm . . ." He lifted his head

42

and laughed hoarsely. "I can't even say it."

"In love," Maria prompted, squeezing into the chair across from him. "It's not a disease, you know."

"Well, it feels like one," he said, staring down at the coffee cup. "It's like everybody else is open season and the one person I want to get with is quarantined. Or maybe I'm the one who should be quarantined," he added quietly.

"Why do you say that?" Maria asked, ignoring Jesse's smirk. She wanted to kick him under the table but was afraid she'd miss and hit Edan.

He shrugged. "I don't know."

"Maybe because every time she sees him coming, she goes the other way," Jesse said from behind the paper.

"Shut up," Edan and Maria said at the same time.

Jesse whistled a few bars of 'Sgt. Pepper's Lonely Hearts Club Band,' a move that nearly earned him a black eye.

"Just ignore him," Edan said, holding Maria's arm until her fist relaxed and she sank back down in her seat. "The worst part is that he's right. I've only seen her a couple of times — "

"Love at first sight," Maria breathed. "Oh, I hope it happens that way for me, too."

"Not if it's one-sided," Edan said, leaning back in his chair. He smoothed his hair into a ponytail, then shook it free. "Wanting someone who doesn't want you really hurts. Man."

The hurt in his eyes upset her. "Who is she? I

want to talk to her. I want to know why she doesn't want you — "

"Easy," Edan said with a ghost of his old smile. "First, I haven't given up yet and second, I'm not gonna tell you who she is because I don't want to have to visit her in the hospital."

"Don't worry, Maria's all talk." Jesse's voice held a smile. "She's never hit anything or anyone in her life."

"There's always a first time," Maria muttered, glaring at his shadow behind the paper. "Do you know who she is, Jess?"

"I didn't tell him," Edan said, sipping his coffee.

"Smart move. Jesse doesn't believe there's any such thing as love." She shot Edan an evil grin. "Boy, I hope I'm around when he falls for someone. I can't wait to rub it in."

"Hey, check this out," Jesse said, rattling the paper. "Some family back in Ohio has a fifty-seven pound turkey that knows how to peck out 'Silent Night' on a piano."

"Big deal," Maria said "Some family here in Washington has a hundred-and-eighty pound turkey who sings lead in a band." She leaped up, squealing as Jesse lunged for her and skittered past, dashing up to her room and slamming the door just as he reached the landing. "Too slow, old timer," she gasped, laughing. "You're over the hill at nineteen."

"You have to come out sometime," he crooned, pressing his lips to the crack in the door. "I can wait."

"Go ahead," she said, grabbing a bottle of Anais Anais cologne from the bureau. Grinning, she crouched, aimed the nozzle beneath the door and squirted.

"Hey," Jesse yelled. "What'd you go and do that for? Now I reek!"

"Yeah, but this time it's not b.o.," she teased, giggling as he stomped off to the bathroom.

She absolutely loved having Jesse home.

Four

"We still have fifteen minutes until the bell rings," Cassandra said, swinging the BMW into a space in the high school parking lot and switching off the engine. She glanced across the car at her cousin. "What do you want to do?"

Natalie stared absently out the window, running her fingertips along the length of one beaded braid.

"Fine," Cassandra said, leaning her head back against the rest. There was no point in pushing it; ever since they'd left Iron Mike's on Saturday Natalie had been acting strange. It had started with their abrupt exit, which had embarrassed Cassandra (how rude to walk out after saying you'd stay) but when she'd tried asking Natalie about it, she'd gotten a sharp, "I did it for a reason."

But she won't tell me why, Cassandra thought, studying her cousin's solemn profile. It had to have something to do with Edan Parrish, but what? Sure, he and Natalie had gotten a little fresh with each other but Natalie usually enjoyed verbal battles. What could have happened to make her panic like that?

And it had definitely been panic, Cassandra thought, watching the sun peek out from behind a fat, gray cloud. What could Edan have done to send Natalie running for her life? My God, she's seen shootings and drugs and heaven only knows what else back in L. A., why would —

"We're here," Natalie said suddenly, focusing on Cassandra. "Why didn't you say so?"

"I did. You didn't hear me."

"Oh." Natalie looked down and twisted her hands in her lap. "I guess I was thinking about something else. Sorry."

Sorry? From Natalie? Cassandra waited, hoping she'd continue and when she didn't, asked, "Is everything okay?"

"Sure." Natalie's voice was loud in the silence. "I mean, what could be wrong?" She hesitated, then swiveled in her seat. Her light green eyes, usually brimming with challenge, were dull with shadows. "I read the letter."

"What letter?" Cassandra asked blankly. "Oh, the one from your mother?"

"Yeah."

"I see," Cassandra said, fingering her pearl earring. This wasn't the answer she'd been expecting and it sure didn't explain Saturday night but she wouldn't push that issue. The fact that Natalie had even brought her mother up was intriguing enough for now. "Is everything all right back in

47

Los Angeles?"

"My mother got a dog," she said finally, picking at a hangnail. "She said it's a little runty thing, a mixed breed she found hiding under a dumpster. She named it Locust because it eats everything in sight."

"That's cute," Cassandra said when the silence had become uncomfortable.

"You think so?" Natalie's mouth twisted. "She also says it's easier to come home now because the apartment isn't as lonely. Man!" She crashed her fist down onto the dashboard. "What am I supposed to say to something like that?"

"Congratulations?" Cassandra suggested weakly, giving silent thanks that her cousin hadn't kicked it instead.

Natalie didn't appear to hear her. "I mean, she sent me up here and now she's freaked because I'm gone? No way! All she did when I was home was rag on me for hanging with my friends and for cuttin' out of that pesthole school. She made my life miserable and now she's acting like the fighting never even happened."

"Maybe she misses you," Cassandra said.

"Right. About as much as I miss her." Her voice roughened and she cleared her throat. "No, I'm outta her way now, safe up here in pristine little Chandler, getting good schooling and staying out of trouble."

"I thought you liked it here," Cassandra said, hurt.

Natalie's look was a mixture of remorse and

impatience. "I *do,* it just burns me that I'm playing the wholesome, whitebread game while she's down in the 'hood bustin' people of color." Her eyes narrowed. "I know why she did it, you know. *She* handed me some garbage about how I was getting dragged down with the wrong kind of people but I know what she really meant."

"What?" Cassandra asked uneasily.

"She couldn't stand that I rejected her white culture and chose to live as an African-American like my fa . . . I mean, my friends. She didn't get it, you know? Not the hangin' wit' the sisters or the hip hop or partying . . . All she could see was 'mug shots and unwed mothers and illegal substances.' "

Cassandra's jaw dropped. "You hung around with pregnant, drug-addicted criminals? On purpose?"

"You're missing the point," Natalie said, scowling. "It's a racist thing; she didn't want me to be an African-American—"

"Hold on," Cassandra said with a spark of temper. "I resent the fact that you equate being an African-American with drugs, crime, and pregnancy, Natalie, I really do. You live with us now; why don't you equate African-American with family, college, and goals? My family works *hard* for what we want; my father poured concrete before he became an architect and my mother cleaned houses before she started selling them. My sister Chelsea's already planning her *pro bono* work once she becomes a lawyer and

49

who knows what Carlton's plotting while he studies all those bugs? *I'm* black and I'm going to be a prima ballerina if it kills me. Why aren't *we* African-Americans? And how can you just ignore the fact that your white mother and my black uncle loved each other enough to get married and have you? Did you ever think that maybe it's not your friends' skin color your mother objects to, but what they *do?*"

Natalie just stared at her.

"I don't blame Aunt Elizabeth for getting you out of there," she continued. "I'm sure most of the mothers in South Central would love to get their kids out of there too, but maybe they're not as lucky as you are. Maybe they don't have relatives with an extra bedroom or maybe they think their situation is so hopeless that they can't even bear to think about it anymore."

"Geez, what set you off?" Natalie croaked.

"Your interpretation of this whole situation," Cassandra said sharply. "Natalie, try to open your mind. If you ever read Malcolm X's biography, you'll see that it's time for us to start taking responsibility and caring for ourselves. Every single one of us who makes good can make it possible for somebody else to make good. We can't wait anymore because everyday we wait, we lose. You know Malcolm's phrase 'By any means necessary?' "

"Yeah," Natalie said. "It always freaks white people out."

"Because they think it means violence," Cassandra said. "But it doesn't. I saw Betty Shabazz, Malcolm's widow, on Oprah last year and she was appalled when Oprah explained that to her. She said 'By any means necessary' means spiritually, academically, whatever it takes to raise *yourself* up, to gain control and knowledge. To read and explore your possibilities."

"I didn't know you liked Malcolm," Natalie said.

"I like a lot of things you don't know about," Cassandra said without thinking. "I also happen to like your mother—"

"Since when have you met my mother?" Natalie interrupted.

Cassandra bit her lip. Natalie wasn't supposed to know about the phone calls because Natalie still didn't know her mother's real reason for sending her up to Chandler. "Um . . . I've talked to her on the phone a couple of times."

"Since when?"

"Since you got here," Cassandra admitted.

"Why?"

"You can't be serious. She's your mother, she *cares* about you! When she didn't hear from you, she just started calling."

"Why didn't you tell me?" Natalie demanded.

"Because she asked me not to," Cassandra said, avoiding her eyes. This was the part she hated. She was a bad liar, everybody said so, and if Natalie caught her now, everything would be in ruins. Hastily, her mind resurrected the answer she and her parents had agreed to give. "She said

51

she didn't want to crowd you. She said she knew you'd call when you were ready."

"Well, she's got a long wait ahead of her," Natalie said grimly. "I can't believe she's been calling behind my back. Man, that's exactly what I should've expected from a cop."

"Oh, stop it," Cassandra snapped. "So your mother's been calling, so what? She's my aunt, I'm allowed to talk to my own aunt. And another thing," she said, really rolling now, "the next time you drag me somewhere and tell me we're going to hang around for a while, *we're going to hang around*. You were rude to someone who did us a favor and if I ever see Corrupting Cleo again, I'll probably die of embarrassment. I may not be as 'cool' as you but at least I don't go around—"

Natalie burst out laughing. "All right already! How long have you been saving this up?"

"Too long," Cassandra said, folding her arms across her chest and staring out the window.

"I can tell," Natalie replied, sticking a finger in her ear. "My head's still ringing."

"Good." Her hands were shaking and her heart pounding. Cassandra wasn't used to losing control and couldn't switch emotional gears as fast as her cousin. Confrontations unnerved her but if this one served its purpose, Natalie would not only be more responsible but she'd also consider making peace with her mother. "There's the bell. Let's go."

"Aye aye, Captain," Natalie said, smirking and slipping out the passenger door. "Hey, it stopped drizzling. Now if only it was Saturday again instead of Monday . . ."

I wish my parents would tell her the real reason she's with us, Cassandra thought, sighing and exiting the car. Sure, she's here because Seven Pines is a safer school and her mother wants her to live to graduate but there's so much more and I don't know if waiting until Natalie feels at home before we tell is such a good idea. I mean, Aunt Elizabeth says Natalie hasn't realized it yet but part of her hostility is pent-up frustration at never knowing the African-American side of her family and, because she had no family to identify with, she'd done what tons of other rootless kids had done; created a fake family out of a gang of friends.

But maybe if Natalie knew her mother had sent her here to bond with her *real* African-American family, Cassandra thought, maybe she'd stop rebelling so much, coming down hard on her mother and idolizing the father she hadn't seen since she was a baby—

"C'mon, Cass," Natalie called, heading for the door.

I'll answer any questions she has, God, Cassandra promised, picking up her pace, only don't let her ask me about her father.

Janis headed down the hall, counting the students wearing dead animal skin coats. "Hmm, seven fur, twenty-eight suede, and forty leather," she said, frowning. "That stinks."

"Picking on my personal hygiene again, Janni?" Simon Pearlstein asked, falling in step beside her. He brushed the ash-brown, shoulder length hair from his eyes and gave her a lazy grin. "I took a shower this morning, I swear."

"Only because Jade wouldn't come near you if you didn't," Janis said, snorting.

"Try again, Madam Oracle. Jade and I broke up yesterday," he said, slipping his long, lanky body between a knot of gossiping sophomore girls and exiting the other side.

"Because she wanted a guy who could remember her name?" Janis said, shooting him a mischievous look.

"Rotten kid," he said to Janis, while smiling easily at the sophomores. "How do you know I'm not heartbroken?"

"Because I know you. Face it, Simon; you've got a ton of animal magnetism but no staying power at all. And speaking of animals . . ." She ignored his groan and rattled off the number of skin coats she'd seen. "And that's only one section of the hall! Doesn't anybody think about what they wear or is being trendy more important than being humane?"

"Why don't you ask them?" He flashed her an evil grin and strolled over to a burly wrestler in a brown suede jacket. "Hey bud, can you answer a question for my friend, here? Go ahead, Janis." He stepped back, eyes gleaming.

"Thanks, Simon." I'll get you for this, Simon,

her smile told him. "Uh . . . I see you're wearing a suede coat, which is made, of course, of a dead cow. Now—"

"Get out of here," the wrestler said, his face turning a dark red. "I ain't wearing no dead cow."

"Yes, you are," Janis said. "What do you think suede is?"

"Well, it ain't a dead cow!"

"Of course it is," Janis said patiently, oblivious to the wrestler's rising blood pressure. "If you want me to split hairs about it, I'd say it could be a deer's skin or a lamb's skin but that one looks pretty wretched, so I'd say—"

"Bye-bye to The Hulk," Simon soothed, taking her arm and steering her away. "Boy, Janis, what'd you want him to do? Throw you down and get you in a headlock?"

"No," she said, smirking. "I wanted him to do it to you. The next time you pick someone to interview, make sure they have a brain bigger than a walnut, okay?"

"Are we indulging in some jock-bashing here?" Simon asked, holding open the stairwell door. "I thought Brian Kelly cured your 'good guy, bad guy, there's no in-between' syndrome."

"It's not the jock clique I object to," Janis said, ignoring his incredulous 'ha.' "The bottom line applies to everyone; if you buy dead animal products, you're promoting cruelty and that means you're not with me, you're against me. Simple."

"Not everything is black and white, you know," Simon said.

"It is in *my* life," Janis said with a shrug. "My parents taught me that a long time ago. It's about integrity, Simon. If you don't agree with the way someone does something, don't empower them by buying their products. You have to take a side and stick with it. I mean, anyone can say they love animals; the question is 'how do they *prove* it?' Do they pamper their poodle and then eat veal? Do they buy their parrot a Christmas present but kill mice? How can *some* animals be worthy of life and not others? Who are we to make that choice?"

"I'm sorry I said anything," Simon said, grinning. "If I'd have known that mentioning jocks—"

"Brian's not your average jock," she said, casting a hopeful glance over her shoulder before entering the stairwell. She'd loitered here in the hall for as long as she could; where *was* Brian this morning? They'd already passed his locker and she felt let down that he wasn't there to give her a smile. "I mean, he worked really hard on the SALS rally—"

"And he ate that miserable vinegar salad you bring for lunch," Simon teased. "What a man."

"You give me a pain," Janis said, refusing to answer his unasked question. How she felt about Brian was her own business, especially since the occasional flirting they'd done had sparked a flicker of hope deep in her heart. It was only a tiny flame but she protected and fed it, using every smile or shared laugh like kindling. Being with Brian was still much too fragile a dream to reveal to Simon, who would laugh and call her an idealistic, closet-romantic. She reached the top step, her clogs clicking like castanets on the tile floor and entered the upper hallway. "Why don't you go find a new girlfriend and spend your time torturing her?"

"Whatever you say," he said with a knowing grin and ambled away whistling G n' R's 'Yesterdays'.

I'm going to do it, Maria thought, leaning close to the girl's room mirror and stroking a thin, black line along her eyelid. She did the other eye then stepped back, examining her make-up. Everything was perfect, from the scarlet lipstick to the light sweep of blush tinging her cheekbones. Her outfit, winter white pants with a cropped jacket and a pair of matching leather boots was new and unblemished.

"I feel like I'm going into battle," she murmured, smoothing her glossy, black hair. Well, if Leif was right and there *was* any such thing as looking too good, she hoped she looked that way now because she needed all the help she could get. Actually, it wouldn't matter if Brian thought she was as homely as a mud fence, as long as he agreed to take her to the dance.

Please God, she prayed silently, I'm not asking

for that much. I don't want him to like me, I don't want to go out with him, all I want is one stupid night at a dance without having to physically pay for it later. I'm not cheating on Leif because we're only seeing each other and he hasn't said anything about Homecoming yet. Yes, I know he assumes we're going together but that's not my fault. I've never brought it up; as a matter of fact I've changed the subject every time—

"Here you are," Tiffany caroled, bounding into the bathroom. "Where have you been? Vanessa's looking all over for you and she's getting really p.o.'d. She had a party Saturday night that you and Leif were supposed to be at and you guys no-showed her."

"Leif never told me about any party," Maria said truthfully, putting her make-up bag back in her purse.

"That's because he probably wanted you all to himself," Tiffany said coyly. "So, have you guys done it yet or what? Can we add your anniversary to the list? That's what Vanessa's party was for, you know. It was two years ago Saturday that she—"

"I don't want to know," Maria said, grimacing. "You tell Vanessa I'll catch her later."

"She's gonna be mad," Tiffany warned, leaning into the mirror and peering up into her nostrils. "Hey Maria, do you trim your nose hair?"

"Bye," Maria said hastily, sweeping out the door.

She had to find Brian.

Janis closed her locker and leaned against it. She had five minutes before homeroom and nothing to do. She could alphabetize her animal rights pamphlets or count more coats but her heart wasn't in it. Something was missing.

Wheeling, she strode down the hall towards the stairs. She'd make one last sweep past Brian's locker. If he wasn't there, her day would have to start without him. But if he was . . .

Good, Maria thought, spotting Brian at his locker. Now all I have to do is ask him.

She stopped behind him, took a deep breath and opened her mouth but the words wouldn't come. What if he said no, then went and told everyone? She'd be humiliated, Leif would be furious, and Vanessa would get off spreading it through the whole school.

Then she wouldn't have any date at all for Homecoming.

"Oh. Uh, hi, Maria."

"Brian. Hi." She felt like all the blood had been sucked from her body. He was smiling but it wasn't a happy smile; it was the same pained one he always pasted on whenever he was around any of the cheerleaders. Up until last week the girls on the squad had thought he was shy and mysterious and a definite challenge but then he'd joined the SALS rally and Vanessa had decided he was a mega-geek. If this fall from grace bothered him, Maria couldn't tell. "Can I talk to you for a second?"

"I guess," he said, shifting. "What about?"

This isn't going to work, she thought. He can't even talk to me without backing away; what does he think I'm gonna do, jump him? "Are you taking anyone to the Homecoming dance?" she blurted and flushed at her desperate tone.

"Uh . . . uh . . . not yet." His gaze lit up. "Hey, Janis!"

"You bellowed?" Janis teased, joining them. Her smile was merry, her eyes bright and her cheeks pink. "Hi, Maria. Nice outfit. She always looks so good, doesn't she, Brian?"

"Sure," he said without looking.

Maria's heart sank. He was doing it again; blabbing away to Janis like some kind of wired, wind-up toy and ignoring everyone else. Why did he do that? Was it the way she treated him, more like a buddy than a prospective squeeze?

"So, how was your weekend?" Janis asked.

"Too fast," he said. "We had a game and I worked. Big deal."

"Boy, they'll never make a best-seller out of *your* life story," Janis said, smirking. "Now I, on the other hand, did all sorts of exciting things, like giving my dogs a bath and baking blueberry bread and meeting with . . ." She paused at Maria's stifled sigh and looked from her to Brian. "Hey, were you guys talking about something important?"

"Just the Homecoming dance," Brian said.

"Oh," Janis said slowly. Her silky blond hair fell into her eyes and she tucked it behind her ears. "Then it *wasn't* anything important."

Brian's smile faltered. "You're not going?"

"What? And ruin my record?" she said. "I haven't gone to a dance at this school yet and I'm not about to start junior year."

"Why not?" His smile completely disappeared.

She made a face. "Because everyone huddles in their cliques, mocking what everybody else is wearing and who dances like a moe, which is probably impossible to avoid considering the lame bands they've had in the past. And don't ask me how I know," she added, holding up a hand. "I may not be in the 'primo' clique here but I still have ears. No offense to either of you two or your brother's band, Maria. Corrupting Cleo'll be the one good thing about Homecoming this year. Oh, and the fact that you're a candidate for queen, of course." She reached over and squeezed Maria's arm. "I hope you win. I'd rather elect Marge Simpson than have any of those other rah-rahs win." She frowned. "Hmm, that didn't come out right, did it?"

"I know what you meant," Maria said, forcing a smile.

The bell rang.

"Well, I'd better run," Janis said, backing away. "See ya."

"Maybe at lunch," Brian called but she'd already disappeared into the milling crowd. He

61

turned, looking surprised to see Maria still there. "Oh. Uh, yeah. What did you want to ask me?"

It had to be now. "Brian, listen," she said, glancing over her shoulder to make sure Leif wasn't around. "I know you're probably gonna hate this but don't say no until I finish, okay?"

"Okay," he said warily. "But if it's gonna take a while, you'd better walk me down to homeroom."

"Sure, great, whatever," Maria said, losing any and all the poise she'd ever possessed. She fought her way down the hall and almost bumped into him when he finally stopped walking.

"Okay, shoot," he said, hovering near the door.

"Well . . . if you decide not to do this, don't tell anybody I even asked, okay?" She waited until he nodded, then crossed her fingers. "You said you weren't going to the dance with anyone but you have to go because you're up for king, so I was thinking maybe we could go to the dance together. As friends," she added at his alarmed expression. "I'll pay my own way and the only thing you'd have to do is maybe dance with me if I win."

He looked at her like she was crazy. "What about Leif? I thought you guys were going out."

"We're only seeing each other."

"So why aren't you going with him?"

"Because I don't want to. Look." She was seized by a sudden burst of inspiration. "If you go to that dance alone, every cheerleader in this school is gonna be on you all night. That's right," she said, nodding at his horrified look.

"But if you go with me, I'll be you're insurance policy."

His eyes narrowed. "And what am I supposed to be to you?"

She met his gaze. "Someone who doesn't expect me to put out when the dance is over." She paused, amazed she'd said such a thing to a guy. If her mother had heard her, she'd have fainted dead away. Too bad, she thought. Desperate times call for desperate measures. "So, is it a deal?"

He hesitated. "Okay."

"Really? Swear you won't change your mind?"

"Yeah." The wary look returned. "Why, is Leif gonna beat me up or something?"

"No," she said, too ecstatic to give it more than a passing thought. She shot him a blinding smile and whirling, took off for her own homeroom.

She was free.

Five

"Slow down, Steph," Phillip said. "I'm not up to racing you to the cafeteria." He tugged her to a halt, pressed her back against the cool, stone wall and gave her a lingering kiss. "Mmm, I'm up to that, though."

"You're always up to that when you're stoned," Stephanie said, trying to sound stern. "Deviate."

"Mmm. Hey, you know what would be paradise?" he mused, stroking her hair. "You and me, alone somewhere with all the food, cigarettes and . . . uh, other stuff we could ever need. No school, no hassles, no nothing but us."

Stephanie wrapped her arms up under his leather jacket and snuggled close, imagining it. They would be lolling on a tropical island, massaging each other with coconut oil and dipping their toes into the warm, lapping waves. Her bathing suit would be a new Ujena, not the shabby old thing she'd worn last summer and Phillip would be even sweeter than usual because there wouldn't be any pot or cocaine in their par-

64

adise. As a matter of fact, the island would be surrounded with voracious, drug-eating sharks that could sniff it out like dogs and had the power to seize it no matter *how* it was being brought in.

"Hot, huh?" he said, nuzzling her ear. "Why don't you call in sick to work tonight and stay with me instead? My folks are gone as usual and we can play paradise."

"Where did they go this time?" Stephanie asked, trying to focus on the conversation and not the shivers racing through her body. "Your parents, I mean."

"Who knows, who cares," he said, shrugging. "Their editors call, they play these competitive little photojournalist games like 'I'm gonna get the scoop before you do' and then they're gone. This one must've been really wicked, because they forgot to tell me where they were headed or for how long."

Stephanie stepped back, sensing his mood had changed. "I'm sure they'll call," she said, squeezing his hand. "Anyway, you still have me."

"But you're not gonna call in sick tonight," he said resignedly, "and we're not gonna get to play paradise."

"You know I can't," she said, touching his stubble-covered cheek. "Now that Alma's gone it's even harder. Corinne and I spackled the walls but I still have to paint before we can advertise for a new boarder."

He sighed. "We haven't been together in so

long that those condoms in your locker have probably expired by now."

"Shhh," she said, ducking so her hair shielded her face. "How could you say that so loud? Did anybody hear you?"

"Hey, I don't care if *everybody* hears me," he said and at her frantic pleas, lowered his voice. "Lighten up, Steph. You know I'd never do anything to hurt you. And remember," his tone grew teasing, "your birthday's coming, so you'd better be nice to me or else."

"Or else what?" she countered.

"This."

Before she could move, he'd thrown her over his shoulder, caveman-style and was striding towards the cafeteria.

"Phillip, put me down," she pleaded, torn between laughter and horror. "We're gonna get in trouble! Don't take me into the cafeteria this way! Phillip, I swear I'm going to kick you!"

"Quit struggling," he said, grunting as her knee caught him in the stomach. "Oof. I don't want to drop you—"

"Mr. Fairweather," someone said coldly. "What do you think you're doing?"

"Hey, Mr. Barnes," Phillip said, greeting the sternest history teacher in the school like he was a long lost friend. "How's it going, man?"

"Put me down, Phillip," Stephanie said in a small voice. They were in for it now; Mr. Barnes had already harassed her for her lack of class participation and if Phillip kept babbling, the teacher was sure to notice his bloodshot eyes and silly smile.

"Sorry Steph, can't do that," Phillip drawled, patting her butt. "Barnes here understands. This is the cafeteria express and we don't drop our passengers off in the middle of nowhere. We honor our commitment to a quality ride—"

"Put her down!" Mr. Barnes's voice cracked like a calving iceberg.

Phillip crouched and Stephanie slid hastily to the ground.

"I'll see you both at Saturday detention," he said, glaring at them. "Nine to twelve. Yes, you too, Ms. Ling. If you have time to play games instead of work on your class participation, then you'll make time to work on it Saturday."

Stephanie shoved the flyaway hair from her eyes and looked desperately over at Phillip, who was gnawing on his thumbnail and staring off into space. "But Mr. Barnes, I work on Saturday—"

"Not this Saturday," he snapped.

"No . . . see, you don't understand," she said, beginning to panic. "I have to paint our boarder's old room Saturday morning and then I have to work until nine that night and all day Sunday. Please Mr. Barnes, it's the only free time I have and my mother's counting on me to paint that room—"

"Then you'll just have to explain why you aren't. Nine to twelve. Saturday." He walked away.

Stephanie's eyes blurred with tears. *"Now* what am I gonna do?"

"Don't worry," Phillip said, giving her a hug. "I'll help you paint it Saturday night. It shouldn't take more than a couple of hours and it'll keep your old lady off your back."

"Really?" she said, sniffling into his flannel shirt. "Thank you. You always know how to make things better."

"Come on," he said, stroking her hair. "Let's go eat. I've got a serious case of the munchies."

She giggled and let him steer her into the cafeteria.

"Hi, Señor Garcia," Maria sang, prancing into his empty classroom. She dropped her purse on his desk, seized the chalk and wrote 'MARIA TORRES WAS HERE' on the board in big, swirling letters. "Beautiful," she said, stepping back and admiring her handiwork. "There, now you have my autograph. Swear you'll cherish it always and maybe I'll waive my customary fee."

Mr. Garcia blinked and ran a hand over his thinning hair. "What're you doing here, Maria? Isn't this your lunch period?" He leaned back in his chair and cocking his head, smiled. "You look like the cat that just swallowed the canary."

"Do you really think so?" she said with an exuberant skip. "Good, because I feel like it, too. I feel like one of those earthquake victims who get caught under a collapsed building and have to wait for days until someone finally digs them out."

"And you've been dug out." His soft, brown eyes were warm and interested. "Has something good happened?"

"Not yet," she said, hugging herself, "but it's going to." She bent, putting her lips close to his ear and whispered, "If I tell you something, do you swear you won't tell anyone?"

"Maria, I don't know if you should tell me your secrets," he said, drawing away slightly.

"Oh." She stared at him, deflated and more than a little hurt. She had been in his class since freshman year, when he was a new teacher out of college and she a lonely student, completely intimidated by high school. They'd become friends after the first class, when Mr. Garcia had discovered Maria already spoke fluent Spanish and considered his class a refuge amidst a frightening schedule. "I thought we were kindred spirits," she said, holding his gaze. "I guess I was wrong. Sorry to have bothered you." She straightened and reached for her purse. "See you in class."

"Maria, wait." His hand touched her arm. "I'm the one who's sorry. I didn't mean I didn't want to hear about your happiness, I only meant . . . well . . ." He made a wry face. "Can you tell me without whispering in my ear? If someone came in, they might think I was giving you all the answers to the next quiz."

"Oh," Maria said again, but her joy had returned. "Well, why didn't you say so?" She laughed and rubbed the spot on her arm that he'd touched, savoring the tingly feeling. "I'm sure you don't want all the gory details . . ." She told him about wanting to break up with Leif — she didn't say why — and about Brian taking her to the Homecoming dance.

"Have you told Leif yet?" Mr. Garcia asked, frowning.

"That's the bad part," she admitted. "I was thinking maybe I'd just tell Vanessa and let him find out through the grapevine —"

"No," he said immediately. "That's the worst thing you could do. It's not only cowardly but it would humiliate him."

"I know," she said, sighing. "I wasn't actually going to do it, I was just *wishing* I could." She made a face. "Leave it to Leif to ruin my excellent mood. I guess it has to be done sometime, so I might as well get it over with now."

"You're a real trooper," Mr. Garcia said with a smile.

"Aren't I?" she joked. "Wish me luck."

"*Buena suerte,*" he said.

"*Gracias,*" she called back, heading out the door.

"What're you, eating for two, Phillip?" Janis asked, ogling the pile of food on his tray. "Tuna sandwich, hamburger, double fries, Twinkies, Doritos, Jell-O and a Three Musketeers bar. Wow." Eyes twinkling, she glanced at Stephanie.

"What about you?"

"I bring my lunch," Stephanie said, holding up a thin, brown bag. "You do too, right Janis?"

Janis patted her insulated bag. "Just call me Old Faithful," she said, scooting around Phillip, who was gazing spellbound at a slice of lemon meringue pie, to give the cash register lady a quarter for a plastic fork. "I forgot to bring my regular ones," she explained to the uninterested woman. "See, I usually carry real silverware because it cuts down on the amount of plastic utensils in the landfills — "

"You'd better move it Janis, or I'll slaughter a pig in your name," someone yelled nastily.

She turned and found Frank Geery and his skinhead buddies at the end of the line. "For shame, Frank," she scolded mockingly. "Talking about your family like that."

"Aw, kiss my . . ." The rest was lost in muttering.

Janis ambled out into the teeming lunchroom, pleased that she'd given better than she'd just gotten. Frank had been a thorn in her side all year, sneering at her vegetarianism and social causes and, while her day was always brighter when he was absent, his harassment didn't have the power to ruin her life. She thought of him as a big, overgrown gnat, constantly hurling himself at a jar of pickles and never realizing he couldn't get close enough to do any damage.

"He must get so frustrated," she murmured and with a satisfied grin, wove through the crowd

71

to claim the empty table waiting at the back of the room.

"That's right, Corrupting Cleo's playing the Homecoming dance this Saturday," Cassandra said, as she and Natalie passed a poster pasted to the wall.

Natalie grunted. "Good for them." There was a lot more she could have said but didn't. Cassandra had been giving her way too many questioning looks lately and her lecture this morning had been freaky. Although she'd only known Cassandra a little over a month, Natalie would have sworn her cousin was just an incredibly beautiful, classy, naive girl who was a magnificent ballet dancer and about as deep as a puddle.

Just goes to show you what a great judge of character I am, Natalie thought wryly.

"Were you serious when you told Edan you were going to the rave instead of the dance?" Cassandra asked.

"Why?" Natalie said, lifting her chin.

"Just curious," she said with a shrug. "I mean, I'm not very fond of rock but now that I know the band members, I wouldn't mind listening to them play. What about you?"

"I'll wait for their first album," Natalie said.

"Interesting," Cassandra mused, toying with her watch. "On Saturday you practically broke my arm to get me into Iron Mike's and now—"

"I don't want to talk about it, okay?"

"Whatever you say," Cassandra said, smiling.

"What's so funny?" Natalie asked, scowling.

Her cousin's smile grew wider. "Nothing."

"You're really getting on my nerves."

"Gee, I'm sorry to hear that," Cassandra said, chuckling.

"You'd better cut it out, girl," Natalie said, rounding the corner to the cafeteria. There was another Corrupting Cleo poster at the entrance and she groaned aloud.

"You can run but you can't hide," Cassandra teased, giving Natalie a pointed look.

"You don't know what you're talking about," Natalie said gruffly, sweeping past her cousin and into the door.

"Hey, you guys."

Natalie turned and found Maria leaning against the wall. "What're you doing?" she said, raising an eyebrow. She and Maria had gotten along okay at the SALS rally but once it was over, Maria had sort of drifted back and forth between the cheerleaders and her new friends. Although Natalie liked what she knew of Maria, she was still leery of Maria's high social status at Seven Pines. "Don't tell me you were waiting for us?"

"No, but I wish I was," Maria said with a sigh. "You didn't see Leif Walters on the way down here, did you?"

"The big blond guy? No."

Maria scowled. "Where is he, anyway? The one lousy time I want to see him and he disappears." She folded her arms across her chest and kicked irritably out at empty air. "Idiot."

"Uh . . . I thought you guys were tight," Natalie said.

Maria started to answer, then bit her lip. She peeked out the doorway and whispered, "You have to swear you won't tell this to anyone, okay?"

"You're breaking up with him?" Natalie guessed.

"Shhh! There are spies everywhere." Maria smiled brightly at several passing cheerleaders. "See you at practice tonight." She waited until they'd left, then said, "I can't stand him anymore. He's so gropey and gross, if I have to kiss him one more time I swear I'm going to throw up."

Natalie looked at Cassandra, whose expression was a mixture of repulsion and fascination. "So, what's the big deal?" she asked, remembering all the guys she'd dumped for pretty much the same reason. And all the ones who had dumped her.

"Well, Vanessa always said anyone who broke up with their main squeeze right before a major event was stupid, so I couldn't break up with Leif till I had somebody else to go to Homecoming with," Maria said, keeping her eye on the door. "And now I do, so it's goodbye Leif, hello Brian."

Natalie went still. "Brian Kelly?"

"Yeah, isn't that great?" Maria said, eyes sparkling.

"No," Natalie snapped, planting her hands on

74

her hips. "I can't believe you'd do this to Janis."

"Janis?" Maria said bewilderedly.

"Yeah, Janis," Natalie said angrily. "And don't tell me you don't know she likes him because I won't believe you. Didn't you ever notice the way they look at each other? Man, I can't believe Brian, either. I thought for sure he'd ask her to this stupid dance . . ." Her eyes narrowed. "Unless it's a status-thing with you guys. Maybe Brian won't ask her because she isn't in the right clique?"

"Natalie," Cassandra said, laying a hand on her arm.

"No." Natalie shook her off. Next to Cassandra, she liked Janis better than anyone else she had met here in Chandler and it burned her that Maria would betray Janis's friendship this way. "She's doing this on purpose, Cass—"

"Stop it!" Maria cried. Her face was pale and her eyes filled with hurt. "You don't understand!"

"So why don't you tell us?" Natalie said, lifting her chin. She listened to Maria's rushed explanation and little by little, a feeling of shame crept over her. She might not understand all of Maria's reasoning, especially the part about not being able to go to a dance without a guy, but it was obvious Maria was telling the truth. Still, she thought, the truth isn't going to hurt Janis any less, is it?

"How was I supposed to know she liked him?" Maria said, appealing to Cassandra. "God, when

I like someone I don't insult him, I'm *nice* to him. All I ever heard those two do was argue!"

"Janis always teases the people she likes," Natalie said, feeling honor-bound to defend her absent friend.

"Well how am I supposed to know that? I just met her!"

"I just met her too, and I noticed it," Natalie said.

"Then maybe you're just smarter than me, okay?" Maria said, folding her arms across her chest and looking away. "Everybody knows how dumb we cheerleaders are—"

"Shhh," Cassandra soothed, sliding an arm around Maria's drooping shoulders. "Nobody thinks that."

"She does," Maria said, glancing at Natalie.

Natalie saw Cassandra's chiding gaze and felt like a bully at the beach. "No I don't," she said, meeting Maria's tearful, doelike eyes. "I'm sorry I went off on you, it's just that I really like Janis—"

"So do I," Maria said. "And believe me, if Janis wanted to go to the dance with Brian, I'd break it off with him—"

Natalie's jaw dropped. "You're not gonna break your date?"

"Why should I? I don't want to go with Leif, Janis doesn't want to go at *all,* and Brian and I both *have* to go. Why shouldn't we go together? Believe me," Maria added dryly, "there's nothing between us. We probably won't even dance together unless one of us wins."

The whole thing sounded logical but something about it still bothered Natalie. "Well . . ."

"I have an idea," Cassandra said brightly. "Why don't Natalie and I bring Janis to the dance with us?"

Natalie's head whipped around. "Huh?"

"It makes perfect sense. I was just telling Natalie how much I'd love to hear your brother's band play—"

"Didn't you hear them Saturday night?" Maria interrupted.

Natalie froze. "How did you know about Saturday night?"

"Edan said you and Cassandra stopped by Iron Mike's," Maria said. "It's a dump, isn't it? They play there all the time though, because Mike gave them their first real gig. I used to go sometimes but . . . well . . ." She made a face. "The other cheerleaders are into pop, not rock."

"Is that all Edan said?" Natalie croaked, not wanting to ask but having to anyway. Had he told Maria how stupid they'd been, lying to get in and then running away scared?

"No," Maria said and laughed. "He said he was direly in love but the girl hated his guts. I never thought I'd see the day Edan gave up his groupies to chase someone who hated him. Man, I'd love to meet her but he wouldn't tell me who she was."

A slow, steady flame began to burn in Natalie's chest, heating her face and turning her blood to

77

lava. She couldn't speak and wouldn't have known what to say if she could. He loved someone? Who? It couldn't be her, she'd only seen him twice, that wasn't enough to make someone fall in love . . . was it?

Don't be dumb, her conscience scoffed. He probably falls in love with someone new every single weekend. And that crap about nixing his groupies; right. What a guy like him says and what a guy like him does are two totally different things. And if he does mean you, it's probably only because he thinks you're playing hard to get. Not because he really likes you.

He *might* really like me, Natalie thought wistfully, then caught herself. What was she thinking? Edan didn't like her; she was just another girl in a crowd of girls.

"That's really interesting," Cassandra said. "I wonder who this mystery girl is?"

Natalie could feel her cousin's gaze boring a hole right through her head but she wouldn't look back.

"So do I," Maria burbled. "Oh, Cassandra, you and Natalie just have to bring Janis to the dance. Everything's going so good and if you guys are there. . . . I mean, I got what I wanted out of this, why shouldn't Janis and Brian? Tell you what. You guys can tell Janis about me and Leif and Brian. I'll be over at the table as soon as that banana comes in and I can break up with him, okay? Oh, what a great idea!" She gave an excited hop. "We can all sit together at the dance, too!"

"Now wait a minute," Natalie said, holding up a hand.

"Natalie," Cassandra pleaded.

"Ease down, Cass. I just wanted to know if it was formal." As she spoke, a bolt of excitement, as hot and bright as lightning shot through her. She shouldn't do this, she *knew* she shouldn't do this and yet she was doing it anyway. I just want to see if this girl he's in love with shows up, she told herself. If I see it, maybe I'll believe it.

"It's dressy but not formal," Maria said, beaming. She looked past the cousins and her smile died. "Here comes Leif. I'll meet you guys at the lunchtable, okay?"

"Good luck. C'mon, Cass," Natalie said, grabbing Cassandra's arm and steering her away. "I can run, but I can't hide, huh?"

"Ha ha," Cassandra said, smiling. "And don't call me Cass."

"I think you should go," Stephanie said immediately, when Cassandra had finished filling Janis in. "I'd go if I was free."

"Since when?" Phillip said through a mouthful of Twinkie.

"Since now I have friends to sit with while you're out messing around in the parking lot," she said, handing him a napkin. "You have crumbs on your chin."

"Why do you go into the parking lot—" Cassandra began, then stopped as her cousin's elbow caught her in the ribs. She glanced at Natalie, who mouthed *drugs,* and her jaw dropped. Phillip did drugs and Stephanie knew it and didn't mind? "Uh . . . anyway Janis, I was really hoping you'd come with us. I've never been to a dance here and neither has Natalie."

"And neither have I and I don't want to start," Janis said, but it sounded like she was weakening.

"Maria said we could all sit together," Cassandra coaxed, careful not to mention Brian any more than she had to. She didn't want Janis to know she and Natalie had guessed her feelings for him, but she *did* want her to know there was nothing between him and Maria. "It'll be fun. Please?"

"Maybe she doesn't own anything dressy," Natalie teased, bumping Janis and gazing pointedly at her faded overalls.

"You should talk," Janis said, tugging on Natalie's 'X' cap. "I don't think I've ever seen the top of your head before. It's probably bald."

"Hey, girl," Natalie drawled, "you saw my capless head at the rally."

"Like I really remember," Janis said, snorting. "I still think you're bald and all those braids are some kind of glue-on suckers. Hey Cass, have you ever seen Nat without her braids?"

"No." Cassandra bit back a smile. According to Natalie, her hair had been wild in L. A., but the braids were a symbol of her new life.

"You guys think you're so funny," Natalie said. "Well, just keep laughing. You'll see."

"Sure, sure, that's what they all say," Janis said airily.

"Okay, wise guy," Natalie said, plunking her elbows on the table. "I'll make you a deal. You go to the dance with me and Cass and I'll take my hair out of braids."

Janis's eyes twinkled. "For the dance?"

Natalie hesitated.

"I knew she wouldn't do it," Janis crowed.

"Okay, for the dance," Natalie agreed.

"Good, then it's settled," Cassandra said, relieved.

"Not everything." Stephanie nodded towards the door. "Leif doesn't look like he's letting Maria off easy."

"Maybe we should interrupt them," Janis suggested, craning her neck for a better view.

"Nah, let it play," Natalie said, watching as Maria pulled her hand from Leif's. "She knows how to deal with him. And besides," she added, tugging her cap low over her eyes and grinning, "she's been looking forward to this for a while. Let her have her moment of glory."

"I thought she liked him," Stephanie said.

"According to what she said, he was . . . uh, very grabby," Cassandra explained, blushing at Phillip's interested gaze. "He made her want to . . . uh, vomit." Ignoring the good-natured laughter, she seized her yogurt and ate until her spoon scraped the bottom.

"What do you mean, 'you're going to the dance with someone else?'" Leif said, staring at Maria. He was standing in front of her and the hand that tightened around hers was hot and moist.

"What do you want to do, advertise it?" Maria said, noticing the cheerleaders nosey gazes. She smiled and turned her back on them. "Listen Leif, we were only seeing each other and you never asked me to the dance and it's less than a week away and I couldn't wait any longer. So I'm going with someone else."

"What do you mean, we *were* only seeing each other?" he rumbled, nearly grinding the bones in her fingers to dust.

Darn, she was hoping he wouldn't pick up on the 'were' part until she was gone. "I just think we should . . . um . . . break up. You're a nice guy and all," she added, trying to be casual as she pried her fingers from his slippery grasp, "but I think you deserve better than me. We can still be friends." And what an insult to my real friends that is, she thought, stifling a nervous giggle. Oh, why didn't he just get mad and storm away, instead of standing there staring at her like that?

"But we were doing okay," he said. "I don't get this."

That's the whole problem, she wanted to shout. You just don't get it! I don't want someone I have to fight, I want someone I can trust!

82

"Look," she said, tempering her impatience, "it was fun while it lasted, okay? There are a ton of other girls at Seven Pines who think you're cute—"

"Sure," he said in an odd, flat voice.

"There are," she insisted, trying desperately to think of one. "Well, anyway—"

"It's over," he said with a slow nod. "Okay. Whatever you want. You're calling the shots here, right?"

"Leif," she said helplessly.

He took a step backward. "Hey, no problem. I know when I'm not wanted. You found somebody else and it's time to get rid of me. No big deal, happens all the time. Do me one favor, though?"

"What?" she said, shivering. His gaze was so . . . remote.

"Promise you'll dance with me when Corrupting Cleo plays 'More Than Words?' You know, by Extreme? I only bought that tape because you said you liked it."

Actually, she only liked it because of Nuno Bettencourt's face but now wasn't the time to go into that. "One dance to 'More Than Words?' " she repeated. "Okay. Sure."

"Great." He gave her a long, weighty look and left.

That'll be the day, she thought and went straight to the pay phone in the girl's room outside the cafeteria.

"Hi, Jess," she said when her brother's answering machine picked up the call. "It's me, Maria. Listen, you guys have to cut 'More Than Words' from your set Saturday night. I can't tell you why right now but trust me when I say it's a matter of life and death. Thanks, Jess. I owe you one."

Smiling, she hung up and breezed back into the cafeteria.

Her body was once again her own.

Six

"You sure you don't want to come back out to the parking lot with me?" Phillip asked Stephanie the next morning. They had gotten to school early and their footsteps rang through the deserted hallway. "I feel bad leaving you here like this."

Then don't, she was tempted to say. What's more important, being with me or getting high? "Don't feel bad," she said instead, stopping at her locker. "I have a story due for Creative Writing and I can finish my Biology homework." She gave him a quick kiss. "You go do whatever you have to do. I'll be here."

"You never hassle me, Steph," he murmured, brushing the hair back from her face.

"I know better," she said ruefully, pinching his butt as he turned to leave. "Sorry, I couldn't resist."

"You're getting mighty brazen, woman," he teased, backing away. "I think those new buds of yours are a bad influence."

Her smile grew anxious. "Oh, no, Phillip, they're not. I mean, I know you think Janis is way out in left field but—"

"I'm only kidding," he said, laughing and shaking his head. "You take everything so seriously. Ease down, will you?"

"Okay." She breathed a sigh of relief. She'd never had a group of girl friends before or felt much like a part of anything and it would have broken her heart if Phillip's objection had been real. She watched as he sauntered away, then gave herself a shake and opened her locker.

All right, Frances, she thought, summoning the short story heroine she used for all her writing assignments. What fine mess are you going to get into today? She took out a notebook and flipped to the page where the assignment had been written.

"Uh, oh," she said, sitting down in front of the locker and propping the notebook on her knees. "This teacher is a sadist, Frances. Today you're going to be in the shower when you hear a strange noise outside the unlocked bathroom door." Stephanie closed her eyes, trying to imagine it.

Hot water. Steam. Ivory soap. Vulnerability.

What would the noise be? A furtive footstep? Or how about the crash of breaking glass?

Stephanie shivered. She hated being scared. She was probably the only kid in the whole junior class who hadn't seen any of the Hell Raiser movies, wouldn't listen to Freddy Krueger's voice, and couldn't look at a photo of Stephen King without shuddering.

I know what *I'd* do if this were happening to me, she thought, doodling Phillip's initials on the top of the pad. I'd faint, so if he killed me I wouldn't know, or else I'd die of fear before he even got into the bathroom.

Frances wouldn't be so lame, her conscience replied. Frances would fight. She'd be on that guy like bologna skin. She'd take that victim crap and throw it right back in his face.

Stephanie tapped the pen against her chin. Yeah, that's exactly what Frances would do, she thought, nodding. Frances was strong, assertive, independent; nobody pushed Frances around.

She bent her head and began to write.

"Hi, Stephanie," Maria said, staring curiously at the petite figure huddled at the locker next to hers. "What're you doing?"

"Writing," Stephanie mumbled from beneath a wall of hair.

"Oh." Maria watched her, intrigued. Stephanie's hand flew over the page and every so often she'd go back and scratch out an entire line. "Well, I guess I won't bother you then."

Stephanie grunted.

So much for that, Maria thought amusedly, opening her locker and slipping off her jacket. She bent, examining her reflection in the mirror on the door and brushed a speck of mascara from her cheek. Was it her imagination or had she always looked so happy?

"Hey, Torres."

Maria's smile died. She straightened slowly and found Vanessa standing behind her. "Hi, Vanessa, what's up?"

"Why don't you tell me?" the cheerleader said, cocking a sculpted eyebrow and ambling closer. "Nice cologne, Torres. You gonna wear it when you go to the Homecoming dance with *Brian?*"

"Maybe," Maria said, forcing back the hurried explanation that automatically sprang to her lips. She would not, *would not* let Vanessa intimidate her today.

Vanessa's eyebrow inched higher. "Oh, we're gonna play it that way, huh? I mean, first you no-show my party, then you dump Leif for Brian Kelly and I'm the last to know. What's with you, anyway? You trying to blow me off or something?"

"No," Maria lied.

"Then where do you get off doing this without telling me?"

Maria lowered her gaze so Vanessa wouldn't see the anger in it. There wasn't any sense in provoking her because they still had cheerleading practice together. "I didn't want to say anything beforehand. I didn't think it would be fair to Leif."

"Right," Vanessa said, snorting.

Maria's head shot up. "Look, you asked me and I told you okay? What do you want to hear?

That it was some kind of big, anti-Vanessa plot or something? He was *my* boyfriend and I broke up with him. There, now you know."

"Hey, don't go off on me, sweetheart," Vanessa snapped.

"Then quit acting like my mother," Maria snapped back.

Vanessa's eyes narrowed. *"You* are getting *way* out of line."

They locked gazes.

Stephanie sat still as a statue on the floor behind Maria, listening as Vanessa's voice grew nastier and Maria's began to wobble. It was obvious that Maria wasn't going to be able to hold out much longer.

"You're so full of it, Torres. Last week you said you weren't after Brian," Vanessa said, "and now you just happen to be going to the dance with him? What do you call that?"

"We're only going as friends," Maria said in a small voice.

"Oh, cut the crap. Why don't you just admit that you were only using Leif until somebody better came along?"

"Because it's not true," Maria mumbled.

"Oh no?" Vanessa's tone turned sweetly calculating. "Then I'm sure you won't mind sitting with us so I can have a shot at Brian. I mean, since you don't want him for yourself, that is."

Stephanie's heart sank.

"I . . . we can't," Maria said. "We're sitting with someone else."

There was a moment of tense silence, then Vanessa's mocking laugh rang out. "Not that bunch of geeks from the rally? Torres, you can't be serious! No, you're sitting with *us*."

"I can't," María said desperately. "I already promised."

"So break it," Vanessa said scornfully. "Promises to geeks don't count for anything."

Stephanie gritted her teeth. If Frances was here, she wouldn't let one of her friends get beat up on this way. She'd stand right up and punch that little brat in the nose. Of course, Frances was a fictional character and couldn't get sued for doing it, either. No, there had to be something else . . .

"Vanessa, please." Maria sounded close to breaking.

Stephanie took a deep breath and squealed, "Spider! Oh my God, spider!" She crabbed frantically away from the lockers and scrambled to her feet. "A big fat ugly spider! Running that way!" She pointed at Vanessa, who had gone pale. "Go! Go!"

"We'll finish this later, Torres," Vanessa blurted and ran.

"Where's the spider?" Maria said, searching the floor.

"She just left," Stephanie said triumphantly. It wasn't exactly a 'Frances,' but it had gotten the job done.

Maria met her gaze and they began to laugh.

Janis pulled her Bronco to the curb on Main Street, grabbed a flier and a hammer and climbed out.

Too bad the phone poles are so far apart, she thought, positioning the anti-fur ad at eye level and reaching into her pocket for a nail. This'll have to be my last one before school or I'll be late.

"You're not supposed to hang things on the utility poles," a querulous voice said.

Janis glanced up and saw an elderly woman edging down the sidewalk towards her. "Good morning," she said cheerfully, hammering the nail in anyway. "Nice day, huh?"

"You're not supposed to hang anything on the utility poles," the woman repeated crankily, squinting at the black and white ad. "I don't have my glasses. Is that an animal?"

"Mmm hmm," Janis said. "A raccoon."

"What's wrong with him?" The woman stuck her face up to the poster. "My goodness, he looks awful."

"That's because he's caught in a steel-jaw trap," Janis said, shivering at the pain in the animal's eyes. She'd seen hundreds of these pictures and they still made her sick. "See that ragged area on the foot in the trap? That's where he tried gnawing it off to free himself—"

"Stop it," the woman said abruptly, looking away. "I know what you are now. You're one of those radical animal terrorists, trying to deprive

91

folks of making an honest living."

You don't have the time to go into this, Janis told herself, then did anyway. "Is it honest when the fur industry tells people the animals don't suffer before they're killed?" She could tell by the closed look on the woman's face that she was wasting her breath but she had to try. "Being caught in a trap is like slamming your hand in a car door as tight as it'll go—"

"Don't compare them to humans," the woman said with a scowl.

"Why not? We both have flesh and nerves and feelings in our bodies, why shouldn't we try to imagine how it would feel?"

"Because animals were put on this earth for people to use," the woman said adamantly. "That's just the way it is."

"Not if I have anything to say about it," Janis muttered, glancing at her watch. She'd have to fly to make it to school on time. "Look, all we're saying is that if people thought about the cruelty involved in what they were wearing or eating—"

"I don't want to hear about it," the woman said, waving her words away. "You people do nothing but stir up trouble."

"Oh, right." Janis's temper surged and although she fought to control it, the words poured out anyway. "It's just easier for you to look at a raccoon coat and see 'luxury' instead of dozens dead, skinned animals, isn't it? Sure, go ahead, believe the fur industry when they tell you how elegant you'll be wearing their 'product.' *They*

want your money, we only want to stop the—"
She broke off as the woman hurried away.

I shouldn't have lost it, she thought, sighing.
Now she thinks I'm a nut and I've only rein-
forced an industry-created stereotype. I fell right
into their trap. Get passionate about a subject
and all of a sudden you're a dangerous extremist.
Darn it. When will I ever learn?

She climbed back into the Bronco and headed
to school.

"Hey, Janis," Brian said on Thursday, jogging
up to her in the hall between classes. "I hear
you're going to the dance."

"That's nothing but a vicious rumor," she
joked, surprised by his sudden look of disappointment.

"But Maria said—"

"Yes, I'm going," she admitted, stopping in
front of her Ceramic Art class. On an impulse,
she held up the wrinkled, spotty, old flannel shirt
she used for a smock. "And I'm wearing this.
What do you think?"

"Great," he said, smirking. "Save me a mud
wrestle."

"Keep that up and I may even save you a mud
pie," she said, returning his grin. "Though actually, it would be a clay pie—"

"A cow pie?" he suggested mischievously.

"Get out of here," she said, laughing and giving him a friendly shove. Was she the one who'd

always thought jocks had no sense of humor?

"I hope you've been working on your point solo for the dance competition, Cassandra," Miss Tatiana said, putting a cool, smooth hand under her student's chin and tilting it up a degree. "Time is of the essence. Have you picked your music yet?"

"I have, actually," she said, steeling herself to hold the *arabesque* a few moments longer. She was pleased at the depths of her muscle control; her back was arched, her arms steady yet fluid and her leg muscles tight and as strong as mahogany. "I brought the tape with me because I wanted you to hear it. It's not your average music but I thought maybe the judges at the competition would enjoy something fresh."

"It isn't rap, is it?" Miss Tatiana said suspiciously.

Cassandra burst out laughing. Her leg dropped and she leaned back against the wooden bar. "No, it's a song I heard . . . well, why don't I just play it for you?"

"We'd best hurry," Miss Tatiana said, eyeing her watch. "The seven o'clock baby class will be in soon with their round little tummies and their eyelids drooping from eating too much dinner."

Cassandra ran lightly to her purse. She removed the Pat Benatar tape, hiding the cover from her teacher and slipped the cassette into the player. "I want you to keep an open mind," she said, turning up the volume and padding to the center of the room. She didn't have much of her routine worked out yet, but parts of the song were perfect for pirouettes.

Cassandra closed her eyes, letting the slow, haunting music slip into her veins and without planning to, she started to dance. She was weightless, borne along on the melody like a thistle on a sweeping nightwind. The plaintive lyrics hurt her heart and filled her entire being with yearning. She was a spirit, floating, dancing, reaching desperately through time for something she couldn't quite grasp, a love so powerful that even in death she couldn't bear to let go.

Her eyes opened but she wasn't in the familiar dance studio. She was lost and alone, roaming the grassy moors by moonlight, searching for a way, any way, to come home . . .

She tasted salt and knew she was crying.

She could not spend eternity alone.

Her soul was reaching . . . reaching . . .

She was so cold.

The music drifted into silence.

Cassandra wiped her cheeks. She felt numb, drained. Even breathing took effort. She lifted her head and met her teacher's gaze.

"What did you say the name of that was?" Miss Tatiana asked, clearing her throat. Her eyes were bright and she seemed to have caught a case of the sniffles.

" 'Wuthering Heights,' " Cassandra said softly, gazing at her hands. They were trembling. "By

Pat Benatar."

"You've seen the movie." It wasn't a question. "The original, with Merle Oberon and Laurence Olivier."

"Many times," Cassandra whispered, savoring the faint music still echoing through her mind. Reaching . . . reaching . . .

"Well," Miss Tatiana said gruffly, "you'd better get to work on that point solo, Cassandra. You have a competition to win."

"Thank you," she said.

"So, how're we gonna do this?" Janis said Friday at lunch. She was picking the radishes out of her salad and crunching them one by one. "I mean, who's driving?"

"I will," Cassandra said. "What time should I pick you up?"

"Never?" Janis suggested with a grin.

"Don't listen to her," Maria said, laughing. "The dance starts at eight, so you guys should be here for like, eight fifteen. Brian and I have to be there a little early, so we'll snag a table. They never, ever set up enough tables. How many chairs will we need?"

"Me, Cass, Natalie, you and Brian," Janis said, ticking them off on her fingers. "Oh, and I think Simon's coming, too."

"And I talked Gus into nixing the rave," Natalie added. "I told him he could sit with us. I hope you don't mind."

"No problem," Maria said. "So that's seven. Good, that still leaves room for Jesse and Edan."

"What?" Natalie said, sitting up straight. "I thought they'd be up on stage, playing."

"They *do* get a break, you know," Maria teased.

"What makes you think they'll spend it with us?" Janis asked, picking up where Natalie had left off when it became apparent she wasn't going to. She looks really shaken, Janis thought, eyeing her concernedly. I hope she's not getting sick. Maybe I'd better bring her some of my mom's herbal tea.

"Because we're safe," Maria said. "Like home base."

"Oh," Janis said, watching Natalie. Her knuckles were white and she was breathing kind of fast. Maybe she had cramps. "Natalie, are you okay?"

Natalie jumped. "Me?" she said loudly. "Sure, why?"

"Because you look sort of funny," Janis said, peering into her eyes. "Does something hurt?"

"Probably the thought of taking her hair out of those braids," Cassandra said swiftly.

Janis caught the look the cousins exchanged and frowned. Uh oh, maybe this bet they'd made was a bad thing. Maybe Natalie really *was* bald, Janis fretted. Hmm, I wonder if my mother has any herbal remedy for hair loss?

"'Course it hurts," Natalie said, sounding like her old self. "And in more ways than one. Do you know how much it's gonna cost to have them

97

re-done? I'll be so broke I'll be eating off all of your lunch trays for a month."

"You can share my salad," Janis said immediately, offering up the tender, organically grown lettuce.

"You keep that nasty thing on your side of the table," Natalie said, making a cross like she was warding off vampires.

"Man, you guys are gonna have so much fun," Stephanie said mournfully, staring down at her half-eaten Spam sandwich. "I voted for you Maria, and I wish I could be there to see you win."

"Then why don't you come?" Janis said, reaching over and squeezing her arm. "So you get off of work at nine and get to the dance by nine-thirty, that's not too late. Come on, Steph."

"I can't," she said, sighing. "I have to paint. Phillip's gonna help me and I know we'll have fun, but . . ." She shot them a 'what can you do?' smile. "Oh well, there'll be other dances."

"We'll have our own dance Saturday night," Phillip said softly, slipping his arm around her thin shoulders and stroking her hair. "While the paint dries between coats."

Janis looked away, suddenly ashamed of herself for making such a big deal about not wanting to go to this dance. At least she had a choice. She glanced back at Stephanie and her friend's watery, forlorn smile nearly killed her.

Seven

"I must've had a screw loose for ever agreeing to do this," Natalie muttered, stepping out of the shower. "Wild hair was for wild times in the hood, not for here." She padded to the vanity, leaving a trail across the plush carpet and rubbed the steam from the mirror. Her long, wet hair hung in spiral ropes around her face and grumbling, she began hand-separating each thick strand into thinner ones. Once that was done, she massaged in a gel conditioner and eased her pick through, tugging out the trillions of snarls.

"So, are you bald?" Cassandra called, knocking on the door.

"Not hardly," Natalie said, scowling at her reflection.

"How does it look?"

"Like beached seaweed," Natalie said crankily.

"When can I see it?"

"When I'm ready." She shoved the mass of spirals away from her face and struggled into her bathrobe. The hair stuck to her back, tickling like a dozen spiders and for a brief, panicked moment, she thought her little cousin Carlton's tarantula Peabody had gotten loose and taken refuge in her robe.

"What're you doing in there?" Cassandra said curiously.

"Practicing body slams," Natalie growled, reaching around in an impossible contortion to peel the hair off of her back. Her elbow banged the towel rack and she let out a howl of pure frustration. "Let me tell you something, *Cassandra*. I don't care if Janis and Brian fall madly in love and run away to get married tonight, *it wasn't worth it!*"

"You sound a little testy," Cassandra said and her voice was filled with laughter.

"You ain't seen nothing yet," Natalie muttered, seizing the blow dryer and jamming the diffuser onto the nozzle. If it was hair they wanted, it was hair they were gonna get.

"I can't believe I'm doing this," Janis said, addressing the animals congregated on the bed. "I bet you guys never thought you'd see me getting ready to go to a dance, did you?"

Isis, the white cat, hefted her hind leg and began washing.

"Charming," Janis said, shaking her head. "What a group." The cats were curled up on the pillows, the dogs sprawled across the comforter, and Star was on the trunk-turned-nightstand, rummaging through a bowl of trail mix. The skunk's body listed slightly, but she seemed to be keeping her balance.

"Janis?" Her mother tapped, then opened the door. "I found that ice pink lipstick you wanted at the beauty supply store."

"Cruelty-free?" Janis said, twisting the tube.

"What else?" her mother said cheerfully. "Try it on."

The smooth, shimmering stick emerged and Janis ran it over her lips. "Hmm, not bad," she said, mugging at her reflection.

"I think it's great," Zoe Sandifer-Wayne said. "Perfect for your outfit. Well, call me if you need anything else."

"How about a psychiatric examination?" Janis joked, tucking her hair behind her ears.

"Relax sweetie, it'll be fun," her mother said, then grinned. "Boy, I sound like Donna Reed. How about this—it might not be the most fun you've ever had, but if you consider it a learning experience, you won't be disappointed."

"That's more like it," Janis said.

"I'll be downstairs making a list of local businesses who might be sympathetic enough to donate to Harmony House." Her blue eyes twinkled. "And I have to warn you; your father is skulking downstairs, armed with a camera and a fresh roll of film."

"Zoe, you traitor!" His shout echoed into the room.

* * *

101

Maria ran her hands down the front of the vibrant purple, skinny-rib dress. She adjusted the mock turtleneck and lifted her arms to make sure she hadn't gotten any deodorant smears beneath the sleeveless armholes. The dress was calf-length, longer than the dresses she usually wore but had a generous slit up the back. She stepped into her pumps, wobbled, then regained her balance.

"Not bad," she murmured, donning a pair of huge, gold rectangle earrings and matching cuff bracelet. "So, do we look queenly or do we just look dumb? I guess time will tell."

"Maria?" Her mother's voice drifted through the door. "You said your date is due at seven-fifteen and it's ten after. If this was Leif, he would have been here already. Are you sure this new boy's coming?"

"Yes," Maria called, spritzing on Opium. Heck, if this were Leif she would be warding him off with Eau de Rotten Eggs, long underwear, and a floor-length Hefty bag. Unbelted.

"But now I'm free." She picked up her purse and walked sedately down the stairs.

As befitting a prospective queen, she thought, grinning.

Right.

Natalie listened at the door a moment, then slowly turned the knob and peeked out into the hall.

Empty.

Clutching the front of her robe, she dashed soundlessly across the thick carpet and into her room. She locked the door and flicked on the light.

She had made it unseen.

Avoiding the mirror, she went straight to the closet and removed a sheer, long-sleeved black bodysuit, an opaque, underwire black bra top and a black mini skirt. Keeping her gaze away from her reflection, she dug tights and a black belt with a heavy buckle out of the bureau drawer.

Humming tunelessly, she slipped off her robe and tugged on the tights. Tonight she would see Edan but tonight she would be prepared, right down to her combat boots. She had thought long and hard about this and had decided there was no use in denying the electricity between them anymore.

All that does is leave me unprepared and then I freak every time he gets within ten feet, she thought, hooking the bra and pulling the sheer bodysuit up over it. Well, not this time.

"Tonight he's got another thing coming," she said, wiggling the skirt up over her hips. If she and Edan had some type of hot, physical attraction going, then the thrill of the chase seemed to fan the flames. Back in L. A. she'd been a fly girl, with feet that could outmove anyone, and if it was a chase he was looking for, she'd run him a marathon.

What're you, nuts? her conscience demanded. You can't play with fire and not get burned! Didn't you learn that back in L. A., with all those slick, smooth-talking guys who said they loved you and then stepped out with other girls? You're looking for a world of hurt, Natalie.

No I'm not, she thought, tugging up the drooping tights till the crotch was firmly in place. I can only get hurt if I care about him and that's not gonna happen. I'm not stupid, I already know what kind of guy he is, so I know better than to believe anything he says. He's looking for a good time and since there's no such thing as true love left in the world, maybe a little fun isn't such a bad thing —

Now I know you've lost it, her conscience groaned. You're gonna sleep with a guy who you know is a slut?

Who said anything about *sleeping* with him, Natalie thought, irritated. I'm talking fun here, not the bottom line. I was dumb back in L. A., but this is Chandler and I'm here for an *education,* right? So, now I'm gonna learn the difference between what guys say, what they're trying to get when they say it, and what they really *mean.* And if I have some fun during class, well . . .

That kind of fun could kill you, her conscience said morosely.

"I said I'm not going to sleep with him," Natalie said, gritting her teeth. "Now, can we drop this whole subject?"

I hope he really is in love with someone and doesn't even notice you, her conscience said as a parting shot. Actions speak louder than words, you know.

"And you speak louder than anyone, so shut up." Natalie rose, wishing she had Neneh Cherry's latest tape, then decided 'Raw Like Sushi' would be just as good. She hadn't danced in way too long and doing a couple of moves in this outfit at home would make sure she wouldn't be in for any surprises on the dance floor. She rewound to 'Buffalo Stance' and pumped up the volume.

"Oh, yeah," she said, giving a few rhythmic hip thrusts. "Girl, you're still there."

Of course, Corrupting Cleo wouldn't be playing Neneh Cherry but sooner or later they'd have to play *something* with a decent beat, she thought, buckling the belt around her waist and jamming her feet into her boots. Now, how to get her black leather jacket and earrings without looking in the mirror? She wanted to see herself as a complete whole, not in pieces, so she closed her eyes and groped her way across the room.

"Jacket." She pulled it on, then felt around until she found the hoop earrings she'd laid out earlier. Now, a drop or two of dark, earthy patchouli oil at her throat and wrists . . .

She recapped the bottle, positioned herself in front of the mirror and opened her eyes.

And started to laugh.

Cassandra buttoned the waist of her rich, rose-

105

colored jumpsuit and straightened the padded shoulders. Critically, she eyed the softly-draped wrap top, then leaned over to see if the V would gap open.

It would.

Frowning, she adjusted the neckline to a respectable depth and pinned it from the inside. She bent again and nodded, satisfied with the small amount of skin exposed.

She knotted the belt at her waist, careful not to wrinkle the fabric, then added her favorite, teardrop pearl earrings.

"I hope I look calmer than I feel," she murmured, tucking a stray hair back into place. Would anyone be able to tell how nervous she was? She'd never been to a school dance before, she didn't even know *how* to dance, which she supposed was pretty funny, considering.

Too bad she didn't feel like laughing.

She cocked her head, listening to the music thumping out of Natalie's room. She probably should have confessed her ignorance and asked her cousin to show her a few steps but it was too late now. And besides, she thought, the last thing I would have needed tonight was Natalie pushing me into dancing with someone and then hanging around to give me pointers. Natalie isn't exactly subtle.

The thought made her pause.

What was Natalie wearing tonight?

Oh, no, she thought, hurriedly strapping on her watch. Oh, no.

" 'Here she comes, Ms. America,' " Janis warbled, mincing down the stairs.

"What's that hideous yowling?" her father joked, covering his ears. "Is somebody stepping on a cat?"

"Ha ha. Hey, I thought you were gonna play *paparazzi,* here," Janis complained good-naturedly, tossing back a sheath of shiny, blond hair. "I mean, what good is being a celeb if nobody cares?"

"I care," her father said, hoisting himself out of his chair and turning to face her. His eyes widened. "Zoe," he called weakly. "Come here. Quick."

"I'm coming," her mother said, hustling in from the kitchen. She stopped in the doorway, open-mouthed "Oh, Janis," she breathed, clasping her hands together.

"Now that's more like it," Janis said, blushing. "Poor Daddy can't even come up with a 'not bad.' "

"Déjà vu," he said, shaking his head as if to clear it. "Zoe, didn't you used to have an outfit just like that?"

"You're looking at it," Janis said proudly, smoothing the pale blue bouclé knit mini skirt set. It was a little tight, her mother must have been an absolute stick when she was younger, and the scoop neck was lower than Janis was used to, but she loved the long, bell sleeves and nubby fabric.

"It looks better on you than it ever did on me," her mother said, smiling. "Maybe it's the blue eyeliner. I don't think I ever wore the right make-up with it. Where's the camera, Trent?"

"I don't know," her father said, dazed. "The first time you wore that outfit Zoe, you had daisies in your hair."

"You remember?" Her mother's smile was that of a young girl.

"How could I ever forget?" he said, touching her cheek. "You were the most beautiful girl I'd ever seen. Still are."

Janis sighed. *This* was the kind of love she dreamed about, not the possessive, game-playing attachments she saw at school. She wanted someone who remembered the daisies.

She didn't need Simon to tell her she was a closet-romantic. She already knew it.

"Natalie?" Cass knocked tentatively on her bedroom door.

"One second," Natalie called.

Cassandra bit her lip, oblivious to the fact that she was scraping off her rose gloss. Natalie sounded a little too gleeful for comfort. Oh, please don't let her have shaved her head just to make a point, she prayed silently, willing to get down on bended knee for the miracle.

The doorknob clicked but the door didn't open. "Natalie?"

"You can come in now," her cousin said.

Please God, Cassandra said silently, don't let her be bald. She reached out and slowly turned the knob.

"Hi, Brian," Maria said. "Come in." She smiled, trying to put him at ease but it only seemed to torture him further. She closed the door behind him, amused at his trapped expression. "Relax," she said, forgetting her social face and giving him the same kind of grin she'd have given her brother. "I swear I'm not going to jump you, okay?"

"Okay," he said sheepishly. "You ready to go?"

"Almost," she said, slipping her coat from the closet. "You just have to prove to my parents that you're not an ax-murderer."

"Actually, strangulation's my game," he said, then turned scarlet as he noticed Mrs. Torres standing behind him. "Uh . . . hi."

"So this is Brian," she said, giving him the eye.

"Brian Kelly," he said, gulping. "Nice to meet you."

"What's your home phone number?" she asked, producing a pad and pen from her apron pocket. "And don't make one up because I'm going to call it. What's your father's name?"

"Uh . . . Bob. I mean, Robert. Robert Brian Kelly." He shot Maria a pleading look. "It's getting kind of late . . ."

"We really have to go, Mom," Maria said, taking pity on him. Leif had been subjected to the same third degree but he'd just laughed it off and later, had told Maria her mother was a real piece of work. Raising her voice, she called, "Bye, Daddy."

The recliner in the family room squeaked and Mr. Torres came into the foyer. "Hello, Brian," he said, extending his hand. They shook and when he stepped back, his dark eyes were twinkling. "You two make a handsome couple. I think we have king and queen material here, don't you, Emilia?"

"Daddy," Maria said, rolling her eyes.

"He's right," Mrs. Torres said, softening. "You're lovely, *mija* and Brian is very handsome. One picture for you to remember this night by." Her hand dipped back into her apron and came out with a small automatic camera. "Smile."

Maria tucked her arm through Brian's, pretending not to notice his sudden stiffness and beamed into the camera. The flash went off, leaving them momentarily blinded.

"I almost forgot," Mr. Torres said, slipping back into the family room and returning with a florist box. "I hope you don't mind, Brian, but Mrs. Torres and I wanted to give this to Maria." He opened the box and showed them the orchid wristlet.

"No, of course not," Brian stammered, sticking his corsageless hands deep into his pants' pockets.

"Thank you," Maria said, hugging her parents.

110

"I'll put it on when we get there. Well." She backed towards the door, strangely loathe to leave their steady, comforting presence. "I guess we're leaving now."

"Nice meeting you both," Brian said, opening the door.

Still, she lingered. Everything was so . . . well, *protected* here and once she stepped out that door, she'd be on her own. Freedom. Suddenly, the word sounded much more ominous than promising. She was free and she had only herself to depend on.

"Maria?" her father said curiously.

"Just taking one last look at my queendom," she said, forcing a light smile. "See you guys later."

Brian held the door open and she swept out into the night.

The bedroom door swung open. Cassandra put a hand to her throat, feeling as though she'd been cast into another galaxy.

"Well?" said the stranger standing in front of her.

Cassandra's mouth opened but no words came out.

The stranger burst out laughing. "Oh c'mon Cass, it can't be that bad. Aren't you glad I'm not bald?"

"Natalie," Cassandra croaked. She inched into the room, clutching the doorframe for support.

111

"How . . . how long has it been since you've cut your hair?"

Natalie shrugged, sending the huge mass of swirling, mahogany-brown spirals into motion. "I don't know, ask my mother the next time you talk to her." She planted her hands on her hips and gave Cassandra a mocking look. "Is that all you can say?"

"I . . . I'm speechless," Cassandra said truthfully. Of all the things she had anticipated, *this* had not been one of them. Her gaze traveled over her cousin's outfit, pausing in shock at the bodysuit and bra top, then was drawn back to Natalie's hair like a pyro to a forest fire. It was . . . unbelievable. Glorious. Wicked. Thousands of gleaming, rippling spirals flowing in all directions, framing a face that was suddenly much too sensual for its own good. That, combined with the outfit (which Cassandra thought had all the class of a skid row hooker) spelled 'danger' in capital letters and if this was how Natalie had looked back in Los Angeles —

"Ready to go?" Natalie said with a devilish grin. "We still have to pick up Janis." She sauntered past her cousin and waited in the hall. "Nice jumpsuit. You look elegant, Cassandra."

And you, Cassandra thought dazedly, switching off the light, have never looked better.

Suddenly, she felt a little sorry for Edan Parrish.

"That's a wig," Janis said, gaping at Natalie.

112

She reached up and slid a hand under her hair, searching for the cap. "It has to be a wig, one of those 'Frederick of Hollywood' suckers." Her fingers inched higher, poking Natalie's scalp. "Come on, *nobody* has this much perfect hair. There's a law against it."

"You thought *she* was bald?" her father said in a strangled voice. "Zoe," he turned to his bemused wife, "I think it's time we had Janis's eyes checked."

Natalie burst out laughing.

"You're enjoying this, aren't you?" Janis said accusingly.

"Yeah," Natalie said.

Eight

"I can hear the music from here," Janis said, following Natalie and Cassandra through the dark, crowded courtyard towards the steps. "What song is this?"

Natalie shrugged.

Cassandra looked blank.

"Oh, we're good," Janis joked nervously, wiping her sweaty palms on her coat. "Our first foray into the unknown and nobody even brought a compass."

Nobody laughed.

"You know, if we leave now we can probably catch Stephanie working down at The Green Café," Janis said, hanging back.

Natalie turned, her green eyes burning with excitement. "Oh no you don't. I gave up a rave to get your butt down here and we're going in. And we're gonna dance."

"I can't dance," Cassandra said softly.

"Neither can I," Janis admitted, plucking at the hem of her skirt. "I mean, I can do all the old

Grateful Dead psychedelic stuff but that's about it."

Natalie stared at them a moment, then grinned. "Then thank God Gus is gonna be here. Now, c'mon." She lifted her chin, tossed back a cloud of hair and strode into the building.

"There's Janis and Cassandra," Maria said, nudging Brian and eyeing the unfamiliar girl standing with them. "Who the heck . . . ?" Her jaw dropped and then she shoved back her chair. "Natalie! Come on, Brian." She grabbed his arm. "Let's go get them."

They wove hurriedly through the tables. The gym was dark and Maria would have tripped over a purse lying on the polished, wood floor if Leif hadn't suddenly appeared and kicked it aside.

"Hey, Brian, Maria," he said, halting her progress. His gaze moved over her, lingering on her chest. "You look great tonight."

"Thanks," she said, well aware of Vanessa sitting only a table away. "You do, too." She'd never seen him in a suit before and was pleasantly surprised. Not enough to go back, though.

"You're still saving 'More Than Words' for me, right?" he said. "Brian doesn't care, do you, Bri?"

"No, go ahead," Brian said absently, staring past Maria.

"So, I'll come get you as soon as they play it, okay?" Leif said, licking his lips.

"Sure," she said, giving silent thanks to Jesse for

agreeing to take the song off the set schedule. "Well, we have to get going. See you, Leif." She smiled, prodded Brian, and headed for the door.

Natalie stared at the stage, watching Corrupting Cleo rock. Jesse, lounging at the mike, flinging his long, black hair and grinding out some song she'd never heard before. Tracer thumping along on bass, his bristly goatee giving him an evil, satanic look and Spec on keyboards, lifting a lightning-fast finger to adjust his horn-rimmed glasses. Dusty, the frizzy-haired drummer with the veiny arms and constant twitch (that only she seemed to equate with being on the needle) pounding out a violent rhythm.

And now the opposite side of the stage.

Oh, boy, she thought, drawing a shaky breath. Nobody should be allowed to look so potent.

Edan's faded, flannel shirt hung open almost to his waist. His jeans were faded and torn at the knees. His strong, square hands ripped across the guitar strings, his tawny hair tumbled over his face, hiding his sleepy, amber-colored eyes.

"Hi!" Maria called, rushing up to them. "God, I'm so glad you guys are here! You look great!"

"So do you," Natalie said, wrenching her gaze from the stage. "Man, that's some dress."

"I could say the same for you," Maria said and laughing, fluffed Natalie's hair. "This is really wild. You should wear it down more often."

"What do you want her to do, start a riot?" Cassandra said, rolling her eyes. "We stopped for gas on the way here and the attendant nearly climbed in the window to get at her."

"She's exaggerating," Natalie said, flushing.

"Oh, no I'm not," Cassandra said strongly.

Natalie started to reply, then stopped. Look, she mouthed, nodding at Janis and Brian, who looked like he'd been sucker-punched.

"Bingo," Maria murmured, eyes sparkling.

"What was the name of that song?" Janis asked when the music stopped. They had drifted out into the hallway, because it was hard to hear over the band. She tucked her hair behind her ear, striving to regain the same friendly, teasing tone she'd always used with Brian, but for some reason it wouldn't come. Maybe because he wasn't looking at her in a friendly, teasing way.

"I don't know." He gave her a crooked smile. "I thought you were gonna wear your mud-wrestling shirt."

She didn't know what to say. None of her jokes or standard, light-hearted insults seemed to fit. "I lied," she said finally, meeting his gaze. "Disappointed?"

"No." His smile turned mischievous. "Actually, yes. I was really looking forward to wrestling with you."

Her awkwardness disappeared. "Well, I'm afraid you're gonna have to find something else to look forward to," she teased.

"No problem there," he murmured.

"Come on Cassandra, let's go back to the table," Maria said, watching Brian and Janis laughing together. Everything was working out perfectly. She had headed Leif off at the pass, brought Brian and Janis together, and was free to do whatever she wanted. She could dance all night without having to worry about leaving a boy friend sulking at the table, or just hang with her new girl friends. And she didn't even care if she didn't win queen. What would the title bring her, anyway? Status? She'd had her fill of status. A crown? She could get one at Burger King if she wanted it badly enough.

"Where's Natalie?" Cassandra asked, scanning the crowd.

"Oh, she headed for the stage a couple of minutes ago," Maria said, taking Cassandra's arm. "Wow, you're not as delicate as you look. There's some serious muscle going here. Did you get that from ballet?" She met Cassandra's puzzled gaze. "What?"

"Do you really want to know? About my dancing, I mean?"

"Yeah," Maria said, surprised. "Why else would I have asked?"

"Maybe to be polite," she said, averting her eyes. "I mean, I know you're kind of stuck with me—"

"Wrong," Maria interrupted, laughing. "I'd say *you're* stuck with *me*."

"Hey, can I be stuck with both of you?"

Maria turned and found Simon Pearlstein grinning down at them. He was wearing a tie-dyed t-shirt, a rusty old black suit jacket, and blue jeans. And he had a fistful of rainbow balloons.

Maria looked at Cassandra and giggled. "I don't know, should we let a guy into our club, Cass?"

"How about a bribe?" he said, plucking a purple balloon from the bunch and handing her the string. "Tie it on your wrist. And for you, the most regal beauty Seven Pines has ever seen, a rose for a rose." He smiled and handed a flustered Cassandra a pink balloon. "So, how about it?"

"Well, he's pretty slick but he *seems* harmless enough," Maria said, giving him a teasing once-over.

"Ouch," he said, wincing. "A poison arrow to the heart. Are you gonna be mean to me all night?"

"Would you mind if we were?"

"Nope," he said with a lazy grin. "It's a small price to pay for hanging with the two best-looking babes around."

Cassandra's eyebrows shot up. *"Babes?"*

"Payback for 'harmless,' " he said, laughing as they each seized an arm and dragged him to their table.

Natalie made her way towards the stage. She wove through the dancers, seeing everything and nothing. Gus was up ahead of her with a girl from his math class. Someone was wearing too much cologne and its heavy, cloying scent enveloped her

119

like a cloud of smog. The music invaded her body, the rhythm seemed to pulse in time with her pounding heart. She knew she was getting a lot of looks but they hit and slid away like rain on a windshield.

"Thanks a lot," Jesse said breathlessly when the song and the clapping stopped. "We're gonna slow things down with something by The Cult called, 'Edie (*Ciao* Baby)'." He swept his damp hair back and closed his eyes, listening as Edan played the intro.

Natalie remained in the shadows. Twenty steps would bring her into Edan's sight range and she wasn't sure she was ready for that. Not with this song playing, not with him singing background about a girl who had the gods at her feet and the stars in her hair. What if the girl he was supposed to be in love with was standing up front and he was singing to her?

Then I'll look like a fool, she thought, straightening her shoulders and lifting her chin. But it's better to look like one now than *be* one later. Onward and upward, sister.

The last few steps were the hardest. She stopped behind a knot of sophomores, bathed in the stagelights' golden glow.

Look at me, Edan, she thought, gazing at him with all of her might. Look at me and let me know if I've made a mistake.

He was deep in concentration, his fingers flying across the guitar strings. Sweat beaded his chest, sparkling like diamonds caught amongst the

120

sparse, golden curls.

Now, she thought. *Here I am.*

He flung the hair from his eyes and glanced up. Their gazes locked.

All sound receded.

Edan went still. Stopped playing.

Jesse shot him a questioning look and sang on.

Although it couldn't have lasted long, maybe no more than a few seconds, Natalie was suspended in time, pierced through the heart like a butterfly pinned to a collector's velvet. She had no breath, no heartbeat. No escape.

Dusty crashed the cymbals. The spell shattered.

Edan blinked. His fingers twitched, then re-claimed the lost rhythm. His gaze never left hers.

Natalie brushed a stray spiral from her cheek. Every nerve ending tingled and the hair on her arms had risen. She was breathing again, she could hear the hushed, ragged sound mingling with the blood thundering in her ears. Dimly, she wondered if she was going down for the count.

The song trickled and died.

"Thanks a lot," Jesse said, smiling at the vigorous applause. "How about some U2?" He shot Edan a curious look, then stepped away from the mike, playing air guitar as the band launched into 'Mysterious Ways.'

"Hey, Nat." Gus slung a friendly arm around her shoulder and grinned down into her face. He was perspiring and lifted his fuschia t-shirt to wipe his forehead.

"Ow, you're on my hair," she croaked, slipping

out from beneath his arm, worried Edan would get the wrong idea.

"Good to see you, too," Gus said good-naturedly. He hitched up his baggy, black pants and said, "Want to dance?"

She started to say 'no,' then stopped. Hadn't she come here to dance? Hadn't she come to let fly, to run a marathon? Well, she couldn't run a marathon standing in one place . . .

"You're on," she said and retreated several feet from the stage. Not far enough to disappear but not close enough to seem like a show-off. She faced Gus, who wasn't much taller than her, and let the beat take over her body.

"Whoa," Gus said with a huge, appreciative grin, trying to match her moves. "You one of Hammer's girls?"

"I'm nobody's girl," she called back, forgetting everything but the joy of the dance. Gus was good too, and more importantly, he was safe. He'd made a move on her a while back, more out of obligation than actual desire, she thought, and although she'd turned him down, their friendship had continued without a hitch.

"Oh, yeah, I forgot," he said, moving in close. His dark eyes twinkled and his hands settled around her waist. "You're the prickly cactus sister from South Central, right?"

"And you like your women warm and willing," Natalie said with a mischievous look. "Like that girl from your math class?"

"She has potential," he admitted, laughing and

122

releasing her. "She's a little cold now but she'll get with the rhythm."

Won't we all, Natalie thought, sneaking a look at Edan from beneath her hair.

He was watching her.

Good.

"We lost Gus," Natalie said, plopping down at the table. "He's chasing some girl from his math class." She gave Cassandra a tired but ecstatic grin and lifted the heavy mass of hair from her neck. She could see the stage from here, could see Edan staring in her direction, but knew it was impossible for him to pick her out of the crowd. "Man, am I sweating." She fanned herself with her hand.

"Want me to blow on you?" Simon suggested innocently.

"It depends on what you had for dinner," Natalie said, lips twitching. "If it was anything in the onion family, forget it."

"M & Ms," he said and leaning over, blew a stream of air on the back of her neck. "How was that?"

"Outstanding," Natalie said with a contented sigh. "Air conditioning that smells like chocolate. Am I in heaven or what?"

Jesse's voice came over the mike. "We're taking a break now but we'll be back in fifteen minutes and according to Mr. Pelham your principal, it's almost time to announce the Homecoming king and queen, so stick around."

"Jesse!" Maria yelled, waving wildly. "Over here!"

Oh, no, Natalie thought. I have to get out of here. She sat up, groping for her purse. "I'll be right back."

"Don't go to the bathroom now," Maria said, drawing several extra chairs up to the table. "It'll be mobbed."

Natalie met Cassandra's knowing gaze. "Some things can't wait." She hurried out, ignoring the figures leaving the stage.

"You said you had a job," Janis said, leaning against the wall and staring up into Brian's warm eyes. "What do you do?"

He shoved his hands into his pockets. "Uh . . . I'm in sales," he said finally. "How about you?"

"I don't have a job now but . . ." She hesitated, trying to measure how well she knew him with what she wanted to tell him. He didn't *seem* like the type who thought AIDS was only a gay or drug-user problem but then she never would have imagined him participating in the SALS rally, either. She decided to go for it. "My parents have started a home for abandoned HIV-infected babies," she said, searching his expression for any sign of disgust or alarm. When none came, she ploughed eagerly ahead. "Harmony House hasn't really opened up yet because we can't get anybody to fund the first year's expenses, but once it does open, I'm going to be an honorary aunt. I'll go there after school a couple times a week and maybe

124

take the kids to the park and stuff." She hugged herself, eyes shining. "I can't wait."

"Sounds great," he said, leaning against the wall next to her. "Will you be on the payroll?"

"I don't know, I never even thought about it. Probably not. If we ever *do* get funded we'd have to pay the professional caretakers first. And besides," she said, glancing up and finding his mouth very close to her cheek, "I . . . I don't think I'd like to take money for giving children love. It doesn't seem ethical."

"And are you always ethical?" His breath stirred more than her hair and the heat from his body encased her like a cocoon.

"I try to be," she said, meeting his gaze. "You?"

"Sure." His voice sank to a murmur. "Do you think it would be ethical to trade one bout of mud-wrestling for something else?"

"If it's a fair trade," she said, barely breathing.

"Oh, it is," he said and lowering his head, kissed her.

A bolt of incredible sweetness shot through Janis. His lips were gentle and his hand cupped the side of her face like it was made of fine china. She felt abandoned when he lifted his head.

"Fair enough?" he asked, smiling.

"No. A mud-wrestling match lasts a lot longer than that," she heard herself reply.

He laughed softly. "You're right."

"I know," she said and lifted her face for another round.

Nine

The line for the girls' room was staggering. Natalie headed for the courtyard.

She burst through the double doors and joined the students out for a cigarette. Although the floodlights were on, parts of the U-shaped yard were pocketed in shadows and Natalie rounded the corner of the building, seeking one for herself.

She leaned against the brick wall, frowning as her hair clung to the rough stone, and wrapped her arms around her waist. She could hear bursts of laughter and the unmistakable sound of empty beer cans hitting the macadam in the parking lot.

"Party hearty," she whispered scornfully.

"Mind some company?"

She stiffened, recognizing Edan's husky voice.

"I tried to catch you before but you move pretty fast," he continued, shoving his hands deep into his jean pockets. The sleeves had been torn out of his flannel shirt and his arms were bare, the fine gold hairs glinting in the floodlights. He stepped out of the glow and joined her in the inky darkness.

"Maybe you were just moving too slow," she said, forgetting her hair was velcroed to the wall and tossing her head. "Ow."

"What?" he said, coming closer.

"Nothing." If she leaned forward to free herself, she would be right up against him.

"I was surprised to see you in there," he said, placing his palms flat against the wall on either side of her. "I thought you were going to the rave tonight, so I didn't recognize you for a minute."

His teasing smile stung, because a minute was all the time they'd spent ogling each other. "Why should you have recognized me?" She put all the attitude she had into her look and ducked out from between his arms, swallowing the prickling pain as her hair tore free. "You've only seen me twice."

"Three times," he corrected, dropping his arms and leaning back against the wall. He lifted one booted foot and propped it against the brick. "Don't forget the audition for your rally."

"Oh, yeah." Like she'd really forgotten.

"Three's my lucky number," he said, cocking his head.

"To me it's three strikes, you're out."

The wind kicked up, ushering the scent of rain into the courtyard and teasing Natalie's hair into a spiraling cloud.

He watched her in silence for a moment. "You really blew me away tonight. Couldn't you tell?"

Not believing anything he said was getting

127

harder, especially since he sounded so sincere. "I don't know you well enough to tell when you're blown away."

"You could," he said quietly, extending his hand.

"I'm not a groupie, Edan," she said, knotting her fingers together to keep from grasping his.

"I never thought you were," he said, dropping his hand.

She was torn between disappointment and relief. If he had reached one inch further, they wouldn't be talking right now.

"Tell me something." Edan's voice was idle but the look in his eyes wasn't. "What did I ever do to make you hate me?"

Hate him? She would have laughed if her throat hadn't closed. She must be a much better actress than she thought. "I don't hate you. I can't hate someone I don't know."

"But you don't like me, either," he countered.

"How can I like someone I don't know?"

"You've got an answer for everything, don't you, tiger?" he said, running a hand through his hair.

There it was, the nickname she thought he'd forgotten. It was dumb, it was trite, and she'd been dying to hear it.

"I try," she said, flashing him a cocky grin.

"Man, what am I gonna do with you?" he said, smiling.

Several answers sprung to mind, none of them repeatable. "I don't think you have to worry about that."

"I don't think I have a choice," he said, ambling

128

towards her, forcing her to retreat until they had once again reversed positions and she was plastered up against the brick. His gaze held her as intimately as if they had been touching.

"Oh, I get it," she joked but it came out a whisper. "You're a stalker and I'm dead now, right?" Her heart was thundering and her stomach a snarl of burning rope. His dark, musky scent invaded her senses, making her skin tingle and her knees tremble with anticipation. He was so close, only inches, a distance that could be spanned with one deep breath . . .

"Natalie." Her name came out low and uneven. "I promised I wouldn't touch you until you said it was all right, remember?"

The promise. At Iron Mike's. One of her dumber moves.

But apparently not destined to be The Dumbest.

He waited, shivering.

"You're cold," she said and opened her leather jacket. "It's all right if we share. For now."

His arms closed around her. The kiss was fierce, hungry, the sensation staggering, but it was still not enough. She buried her hands in his hair, urging him closer. She could feel his heart pounding, feel the scorching heat of his body —

"Well, look at that," someone said disgustedly. "Check it out, guys. Corrupting Cleo's guitar player likes Oreos."

Natalie froze, feeling as though she'd plunged through a hole in the ice. An Oreo. A racist term that brought back waves of humiliation, anger, and

129

sick, stomach-turning dread.

"Hey, don't they say once you go black, you never go back?" Frank Geery, the only skinhead Natalie recognized, sneered.

The rest of the gang laughed.

Edan's body shielded her from the taunting group. "Ignore them," he murmured. "If we don't react, they'll go away."

She wanted to believe him. She wanted to bury herself in his arms and hide until they left but she just wasn't made that way.

"Hey, Frank," a fat girl in fatigues said loudly, "isn't she the one who hangs out with that veghead? You know, the one who saves bunnies and Bambis?"

"And now cookies?" someone else cracked, setting them off.

Natalie went rigid. "That does it," she said, trying to struggle out of Edan's embrace. "Let me go!"

"Wait," he muttered, trapping her against him. "What're you gonna do, fight all of them?" He looked at Frank and snapped, "Why don't you bunch of bozos give it a rest?"

"Our school," Frank said, shrugging. "We don't like—"

Edan's eyes turned to stone. "Get out of here," he said in a low, deadly voice. "Now."

The skinheads exchanged glances, then smirking, sauntered nonchalantly back towards the parking lot.

Edan looked at Natalie. "Are you okay?"

"Fine," she said abruptly, slipping out of his embrace. She couldn't meet his eyes, couldn't stay with him another second. She wanted to, but couldn't.

He took a step towards her, stopping as she backed away. "Nat? What's wrong?"

Her heart hurt. " 'For now' is over, Edan. It was fun while it lasted but it's time to get back to the real world."

"Aren't we real?" he asked.

"There is no 'we,' " she said and left.

Innocently, Maria opened her mouth to tease Natalie about her and Edan's coincidental disappearance but the look on Natalie's face stopped her. She glanced worriedly at Cassandra, who stared helplessly back.

The band started up. The song was fast, hard-edged and Edan's guitar riffs grated like a file against Maria's spine. This was the darkest, angriest version of G n' R's 'Welcome to the Jungle' she'd ever heard.

What the heck happened, she wondered. The band goes on break. Natalie beelines for the bathroom. Edan disappears. No one can find either one of them and suddenly Natalie's here looking like she's dying and Edan's up there ravaging his guitar . . .

Her jaw dropped. Edan and Natalie? Could Natalie be the one? She looked at Cassandra, who blushed and averted her gaze.

"I want to dance," Natalie said suddenly, glaring at Simon.

"How can I say no to such a charming invitation?" he said good-naturedly and followed her out to the dance floor.

"He has no idea what he's in for," Cassandra said, watching her cousin surround Simon with a fierce, desperate energy.

"Cassandra, what do you think happened?" Maria asked.

"Don't ask," she said quietly.

Troubled, Maria leaned on her elbows, watching as Natalie performed the darkest, angriest dance of her life.

"We should go back inside," Janis said, smiling up at Brian. "I mean, this is my first Seven Pines 'do' and I'm spending the whole thing in the hall."

"I guess we have to, huh?" Brian said reluctantly.

"Yes, duty calls," she teased.

"Before we go back . . . do you think we could like, start seeing each other or something?"

"What's the 'or something?' " she said and laughing, gave him a quick kiss. "I think it could be arranged."

Maria sat at the table, contentedly watching her friends out on the dance floor. Slow dancing was the one thing she needed a partner for but the spare guys had all been taken. Cassandra and Simon were laughing, not looking in the least romantic and Janis and Brian had stars in their eyes. Natalie and Gus were swaying in time to the music. Corrupting Cleo had followed up with G n' R's 'Don't Cry' and now Edan's guitar was moaning in anguish.

"Maria?" Leif appeared beside her. "Wanna dance?"

"Uh . . . I thought we were waiting for that Extreme song," she said, folding her arms across her chest to dislodge his gaze.

"I don't think they're gonna play it," he said, meeting her eyes. "I asked your brother and he said it wasn't in the set."

"Oh." Maria could have kicked Jesse. Why hadn't he used his brain and said he'd try to fit it in, instead? "Well . . ."

"C'mon," he said quietly. "What's one dance?"

She rose, wishing she had the nerve to just say no. "All right, but this isn't gonna change anything. We're only friends."

"You're calling the shots," he said, taking her hand.

She accompanied him to the dance floor, uneasy at the small, secret smile playing on his lips.

Every word Edan sang tore another hole in Natalie's heart. His deep voice blended with Jesse's, painting the lyrics with pain and yearning and husky, whispered pleas.

"Hey, you're not supposed to take it seriously,"

Gus joked, reaching up and wiping a stray tear from her cheek. "It's only a song, Nat. They don't really mean it."

"I know." She rested her head on his shoulder and gazed at the stage. "I know."

"And now, the moment you've all been waiting for," Jesse said, grinning at the crowd. "Mr. Pelham, your principal and mine, will announce the Seven Pines Homecoming King and Queen."

Mr. Pelham strode across the stage. "Thank you, Jesse," he said into the mike. "It's good to finally see you and Mr. Parrish in gym."

"They almost failed for cutting it," Maria said, laughing and leaned around Brian to Janis. "Hey, if I win, can I borrow Brian for a dance?"

"Sure," Janis said, eyes twinkling.

"Don't I have anything to say about this?" Brian joked.

"Not anymore," Simon said, sipping a can of Coke.

Maria shot Simon a mischievous grin. "Forget Brian. If I win, I want to dance with *you*."

Simon groaned. "Have a heart, Maria. I'm no good at this social stuff."

"If you don't dance with the queen, she'll have you beheaded," Maria said sweetly.

"Too bad Halloween's gone," Janis said, smirking at Simon. "I could have used a ready-made jack o'lantern."

"This year's Homecoming Queen is . . ." Mr. Pelham unfolded a slip of paper. "Maria Torres. Come on up, Maria."

"Oh," she said, blushing, laughing and feeling ridiculously happy at her friends' good wishes. She motioned to Simon. "I'll have to dance with the King first but then it's your turn, sailor."

Smiling, she walked to the stage. The balloon tied to her wrist was bobbing like a wild thing, drawing friendly laughter.

"Nice job, *mija,*" Jesse said, giving her a big hug.

"Congratulations, Maria," Mr. Pelham said, placing a gaudy, paper maché crown studded with plastic jewels atop her curls. "The Homecoming King is . . . Brian Kelly."

Brian mumbled "Thanks," when Mr. Pelham crowned him.

"You hate this, don't you?" Maria whispered, as they took their places on the dance floor.

"Yeah," he said, running a finger around his shirt collar.

"Well, how about if I brighten your day?" she said, moving easily in his awkward embrace. "Why don't you take Janis home instead of me? I'll grab a ride with someone else."

His eyes lit up. "Really? You wouldn't mind?"

"No," she said, laughing. "Oh, Mr. Pelham's signaling. It's time to dance with our dates."

Brian didn't say it aloud, but his expression spoke for him.

Outstanding.

"Your jock buddies got a little weird when they saw me coming out here to dance with you," Janis said, drawing back to study his face. "The blond,

Vanessa, even booed."

"Vanessa's a waste of valuable oxygen," he said. "Janis, Maria said it was okay if I took you home. She's gonna catch a ride with somebody else. What do you think?"

"Are you sure she doesn't mind?"

"She was the one who suggested it," he said, pulling her close and resting his cheek against her hair.

"Okay, then," Janis said, smiling.

"Your servant, madam," Simon drawled, making a sweeping bow out in the middle of the dance floor.

"Arise, knave," Maria said, poking the top of his head and laughing so hard she forgot all about asking him for a ride home.

"This night really flew," Cassandra said later, standing with Natalie out in the hall by the soda machine. They'd deserted their table after the guys had left and Maria had been swept into the jock crowd for congratulations. "Simon's nice, isn't he?"

"He's okay," Natalie said. "Why didn't you go to that rave with him and Gus?"

"And how would you have gotten home?"

She shrugged. "Me and Janis could've hitched a ride with Maria and Brian."

"Brian's taking Janis home. Good instincts, Natalie."

"My instincts stink," she muttered, averting her eyes. "So, how's Maria getting home?"

"I think we're taking her—" Cassandra began.

"I'm giving her a ride."

Natalie glanced up into Leif Walter's face. He was standing by the soda machine, palming two cans of Coke. "Since when?"

"Since a couple minutes ago," he said stonily.

"Okay," Natalie said distractedly, glancing at her watch. It was almost eleven o'clock, the dance was ending, and the faint sound of Edan's guitar was haunting her like a wraith. "Come on then Cass, let's go."

"Don't you want to stay to the end?" Cassandra said.

And be here when Edan was free to leave the stage? "No," she said, as the music died and Jesse's voice came over the mike. "No, let's go. Now. Come on."

"But we haven't said goodbye to anyone—"

"Cass, please. Leif's taking Maria home, there's no reason to stay. Please?"

Cassandra nodded. "Let's go."

They hurried down the corridor and out the courtyard doors.

"Thanks a lot, Jesse," Maria said, lingering on stage. The gym was nearly deserted and still Natalie hadn't appeared. She looked at Edan, who was sitting slump-shouldered in front of the drumset and sighed. She'd stayed as long as she could, hoping to lure Natalie in, but it obviously hadn't worked. "Well, I better get going." Still wearing her crown, she made her way carefully down the stage steps. "Goodnight, you guys. Nice job."

"Where's your ride, *mija?*" Jesse called absently.

"Probably waiting in the parking lot," she said, heading for the back door that led out to the parking lot. Her footsteps echoed and she pulled on her coat as she walked. She *had* asked Cassandra for a ride, hadn't she? she thought, trying to remember. Yeah, she'd yelled her request right before Vanessa had dragged her away, pretending to be thrilled for her. What a crock. And what a relief it was, knowing she was now free to hang around with the people she wanted instead of the people she was *supposed* to.

"I hope she's parked close by, because these shoes weren't made for rain." She hit the bar and the heavy door swung open.

Instantly, a pair of headlights went on in the back row.

"Over here," she said, waving and letting the door slam behind her. She held a hand over her crown, trying to protect it from the cold rain and watched the car circle around towards her. That doesn't look like Cassandra's BMW, she thought. That looked like a Trans-Am . . .

Leif rolled down the passenger window. "Need a ride?"

"Thanks anyway, but Cassandra's around here somewhere —"

"She left a half hour ago," he said, shaking his

138

head.

"Oh." She frowned. Why would they have left without her?

"Come on, I'll take you home." He opened the passenger door.

She took a step backwards. "Wait, I'll see if my brother can. I don't want you to go out of your way." She yanked on the gym door but it wouldn't budge.

"They lock them from the inside," he said, watching her.

"Oh." She squinted into the rain, wondering if she should hike all the way around the building to the courtyard. Would that door still be open or had they locked it, too?

"C'mon, Maria." Leif sounded hurt. "It's only a ride home. What do you think I'm gonna do, kidnap you or something?"

She hesitated, then gave in. What *could* he do? Ask her to go out? "Sorry," she said, smiling and slipping into the warm, dry car. "Us queens have to be careful, you know."

"Right," he said, watching as she pulled the door shut.

"Ready?" she said, buckling her seat belt. His unwavering gaze made her uncomfortable and she closed her coat.

"Let's do it," he said and barreled out of the parking lot.

They drove in silence for a while and Maria relaxed, lulled by the windshield wipers' rhythmic swooshing and the tires steady hum on the wet pavement. It had been a wonderful night.

"Want to stop somewhere for a cup of coffee?" Leif asked, turning off of Main Street and taking the road past the park.

"Oh, no. Thanks anyway, but I'm pretty exhausted," she said, watching the thick woods blur by. He was taking the long way to her house and she felt kind of bad for his wanting to prolong things this way.

"I wonder why you're exhausted," he said in an odd, flat tone. "Maybe you're seeing too many guys, huh?"

The hair on the back of her neck prickled. "Leif," she said firmly, sitting up straighter, "it's been a long day and I don't really feel like—"

"Who cares?" He wrenched the wheel, sending the Trans-Am screaming down an overgrown lane. Branches lashed the windows, slapping and screeching along the car, their naked, brown fingers like skeletons groping for salvation. "Who cares what *you* feel like? It's *my* time now. What about how *I* feel? What about what *I* want?" He slammed the car into 'park' and killed the ignition.

"Wh . . . what are you doing?" Maria stammered. Her crown had tumbled off and lay on the floor, forgotten.

"I'm taking," he began ominously, reaching over and with slow, deliberate movements, unbuckling her seatbelt, "what you gave Brian and the balloon man and everybody but me. I'm not waiting anymore."

She stared at him, confused. What had she given

Brian and Simon tonight that she hadn't given Leif? Nothing. She'd danced with all three—

He unzipped his pants.

No, she thought, reeling as the true meaning of his words hit her. This can't happen. We're not even going out. I don't love him, I don't even *like* him. He can't be serious. No.

"Don't even think about running away," he said, wetting his lips. He straddled the console, pressing his leg against hers and towered over her like a huge, menacing mountain. "I could tackle you before you get ten feet." He smiled, watching her face. "Now . . ."

"Leif, no." Her entire body was trembling and raw terror rained down, crushing her like a landslide. "Don't. This isn't right, I'm not that way—"

"Yes, you are," he said, grabbing a handful of her hair and jerking her towards him. He buried his face in her neck, mouthing her ear, her cheek, shoving back her coat to get to her shoulder. "You're a tease, you go smiling and wearing these kind of clothes just to get guys hot . . ." His eyes glistened with anger. "I spent more time and money on you than anybody else and I'm the only one who hasn't gotten anything."

"No," she whimpered, trying to push him away. He was heavy, so heavy, and his hot breath made her gasp for air. His hands were everywhere, cruel hands, hurting her, hating her, making her want to scream until her throat was raw.

"Oh, yeah." His voice was ragged.

"Stop," she cried, squirming until her back was

141

against the passenger door. "Please Leif," she panted as he hovered over her, "don't do this. Don't hurt me. I'm not that way, I've never—"

"Shut up," he growled.

"Please," she said, starting to sob. "I'm not a tease—"

"Shut up!" He slapped her. Once. Hard.

Her head smacked the window, sending spears of hot, white light into her brain. Her teeth sliced through her bottom lip. She stared at him, shocked. And then the pain bloomed.

"Just shut up," he warned in a quieter voice.

"Ow, ow, ow," she blubbered, holding the side of her face. "How could you hurt me? My mother *liked* you."

"Shut up." His hands gripped her knees.

"My mother liked you." The words rasped out of her aching throat like a chant. She couldn't stop saying them, couldn't stop crying. Her nose was running, her mouth dripping blood and still she couldn't stop. He would hit her again and still she would cling to the words. "My mother liked you."

He drew back, his lip curled in disgust. "Go," he said roughly. "You're not worth it."

She blinked, not understanding him.

"You'd probably give me some disease," he said, staring at the mucus, blood, and tears smearing her face. "Get out of here. *Now.*"

Hiccupping, she fumbled for the door handle. Her hair fell in her eyes, she couldn't see and when she finally found it, she couldn't make it work. It was too much. She freaked, pounding her fists on the window.

The door opened and she pitched out, sprawling in the mud.

"Don't forget your crown," he said mockingly, tossing it out. He slammed the door, fired up the engine, and drove away.

Ten

"The dance must be over by now," Stephanie said wistfully, lowering the radio. She rubbed her nose, smearing the white paint splattered across it and sighing, knelt to run the roller through the paint pan. "I bet they had a really good time."

"Didn't you have a good time dancing with me?" Phillip asked, resting his brush on the can and taking her in his arms.

"Yeah," she said, snuggling into him. "If you hadn't been here, I would've died. You always make everything good for me."

"Everything?" he asked wickedly.

"Shhh," she said, blushing and glancing back at the door in time to see a shadow swiftly disappear. "Darn it."

"Who was it this time; Corinne, Anastasia, or your old lady?" Phillip said, releasing her.

"Corinne doesn't sneak, so it was either Anastasia or my mother," she said, crossing the room and peering into the hall. As she'd suspected, it was empty. "I wish you hadn't told Ana she looked cute in all that make-up," she added, rescuing her roller before it was submerged in paint. "She's only thirteen, Phillip."

"If you think that's bad, then I'd better never tell you what *I* was doing at thirteen," he said, sounding irritated. "Come on Steph, lighten up. She's only a kid."

"We know that but she doesn't," Stephanie said, pressing a hand to her back. "I'm so tired. First detention, then work, and now this. Am I being punished for something or what?" She'd meant it as a joke and was surprised at Phillip's sharp response.

"Hey, if you don't want me here I can leave, you know," he said, plopping the brush into the can and slopping paint onto the newspapers. "I mean, this ain't no picnic for me, either."

"You know that's not how I meant it —" she began.

"I could be home partying or hanging with Jared." Scowling, he searched the floor as if looking for something to kick.

"I know," she said, hurrying to his side. "And I really appreciate you giving up a Saturday night to help me." She stood on tiptoe and pressed a kiss to his unresponsive lips. "Better?"

"Sure," he said, brushing her away. "I'll be right back."

"You're going out to your bike *again?*" She regretted the words as soon as she said them.

"Yeah, *again.* I gotta have some kind of fun tonight." He wiped his nose on his forearm, withdrew a small mirror and a rolled up bill from his

145

pocket, and stomped out of the room.

Where are all the drug-eating sharks when I need them, she wondered miserably, gathering up the paint-splashed papers.

"Want to come in for a while?" Janis said dreamily, resting her head on Brian's shoulder. They were sitting in his pick-up in her driveway, watching the rain trickle down the glass. "I could make us some herbal tea."

"How about coffee?" Brian said, pressing a kiss to her hair.

"I think we have some decaf we keep for company." If she lived to be a hundred, never, *ever* would she forget this magical night. Now I know how flowers feel when spring finally comes, she thought, curling her fingers through his. "Come on, you can meet my family." She grinned. "How do you feel about skunks?"

"They make ugly coats," he joked.

Her smile died. "Don't ever say that. We rescued Star from one of those hideous, steel-jaw traps, Brian. She was almost dead and we had to have her foot amputated—"

"Okay, sorry," he said. "Give me a break, will you?"

"I'm sorry too. I shouldn't have gone off on you like that. See, I have this really bad temper that I can control pretty well but I guess I should warn you," she said smiling, eager to return to their earlier bliss, "there are a few of my buttons you don't want to push. Now, let's go in—"

"Jan?" He played idly with her fingers. "Maybe another time, okay? I don't think I'm up to doing the 'family thing' tonight."

"Oh." She was hurt. Her family was everything to her and she wanted it to be everything to him, too. Maybe I'm rushing it, she thought. Am I turning into one of those awful girls I see at school, clinging to their boyfriends like ivy? "Okay."

"You're not mad, are you?" he asked.

"No, smiley, I'm not mad," she said. "But I *will* be if you don't give me one last kiss for the road."

"I'm the one who's gonna be on the road," he said.

"Then I'll have to give you one, too."

"Is that you, girls?" Mrs. Taylor called as the cousins stepped into the foyer. "Come on in and tell us about the dance."

Natalie grimaced. "Not me, Aunt Miriam. I'm going to bed."

"But it's only eleven-thirty." Her aunt glided into the room, carrying a porcelain tea cup and when she saw Natalie, nearly dropped it. "Sweet Lord," she said faintly, closing her eyes. "Don't tell me you wore that out in public."

"Yup," Natalie said, in no mood for a lecture.

"She was a big hit," Cassandra said hurriedly, hanging her coat in the closet. "We had a nice time, Mom. Our friend Maria won Homecoming Queen and I even danced."

"Well of course you did," her mother said, still

147

staring in horror at Natalie. "You're a dancer, why shouldn't you dance?"

"Miriam?" Mr. Taylor's voice rumbled in from the den. "Is everything all right?"

"Yes, Daddy," Cassandra called before her mother could speak. "Mom, we're going upstairs now. Good night." She gave Natalie a push and whispered, "Go! My father will burn those clothes before he'll let you wear them again."

Natalie hesitated, ripe for an argument. "Good night, Aunt Miriam," she said finally and followed Cassandra upstairs.

What am I going to tell my parents? Maria wondered, plodding along the side of the road. She wasn't crying anymore; her tears had dried up half a mile ago and a sort of numb acceptance had settled over her. She was a tease and therefore, she should have expected this. She deserved to be cold and wet and stranded in the rain. Leif was right. No girl with big breasts should flirt or wear ribbed dresses or be Homecoming Queen. It was her fault for looking too good, just like he'd said a million times before.

Well, she didn't look so good now. She touched her swollen, bottom lip. It wasn't bleeding anymore and from what she could see in her compact, the rain had washed away the blood. She had searched the side of her face for a bruise and when she'd found nothing, kept her cheek tilted up as she walked, praying the cold rain would take care of that, too. There was nothing she could do about

148

her shoes but carry them, which made walking harder on her feet but faster. Her hair was drenched, her coat a hundred-pound sponge and she had no feeling left in her fingers or toes.

Maybe I'll say I got in a car accident, she thought. No, no good. Her mother would be sure to phone the police for details.

And then she'll take me to the hospital and the last thing I want is for someone professional to see me. . . . Gritting her teeth, she fought back the tears. They'll look at me and know what I am and they'll tell my parents and I won't ever be able to look at them again. Oh, God, I'm so ashamed.

She walked on, taking side streets instead of main ones to avoid cars. Anyone could be Leif, looking to start up where he'd left off . . . or worse, Vanessa, who'd jump at the chance to spread the word.

"I know what I'll say. I'll tell them the truth about Brian and Janis and then say I hitched a ride with some kid from school with a junky old car and it broke down and I decided to walk home because it wasn't that far and I cut through the park and fell." She laughed but the sound held no amusement. "At least it won't be a total lie and anything's better than the truth."

She turned down her street. Her parents had left the porch light on and it shined like a beacon, guiding her home.

She started to run.

* * *

Natalie stood in the bathroom, staring at her reflection.

"Oreo," she said in a flat voice, watching her lips release the hated word. "Surprise surprise, Natalie. Even here in pristine little Chandler you can find hate. And you thought you could start over, be an African-American." She laughed harshly. "Who are you kidding? No matter where you go or what you do, you'll always be nothing but an Oreo. The brothers in South Central knew it and the skinheads in Chandler know it. Why don't *you* know it?"

She grabbed a clump of hair and started braiding. It wouldn't be a professional job but it would be done and once it was done, she would never think of this night again.

"Hi," Maria called, stepping into the foyer. Warmth enfolded her like a soft, familiar blanket and she swallowed hard, bracing herself. "I'm home."

"Hi, honey," her father called from the family room. "Did you have a nice time?"

"Yeah," she said, waiting nervously for her mother to come bustling in. "Jesse's band was great, as usual. Where's Mommy?"

"Taking a shower," her father said.

She heard his newspaper rattle and couldn't quite believe her good luck. "Then I'm gonna get out of this outfit. My feet are killing me." She waited and when he didn't add anything, had a burst of inspiration. "Can you take my coat into the cleaners with you Monday? We were kind of hanging around outside in the rain for a while and it's pretty wet."

"Sure," he said. "Leave it where I can find it."

"Thanks. Oh, and do we have an ice pack? I tripped in these dumb high heels and split my lip. It was so embarrassing." She held her breath, wondering if he'd accept her explanation.

"You okay?"

"Yeah. No big deal."

"Well, the ice-pack's in the freezer. And throw those darn shoes away," he added. "I told you they were too high."

She sagged against the bannister. "I know. I'm going to." He must've forgotten all about Homecoming Queen, which was good because she'd left the crown where Leif had tossed it.

She padded upstairs and past the main bathroom. The door was closed and the water running. So far, so good.

Please God, she prayed silently, closing her door and dropping the sodden coat, let me get through this without them finding out. Please. She peeled off the dress and the ruined stockings and stuffed them under the bed to dispose of later. She slipped on her robe and headed for the other shower. Once inside, she soaped and scrubbed until her fingers were pruny.

She didn't feel clean but there was no changing that.

* * *

Janis breezed into the house and shook herself, sending iridescent raindrops winging across the floor. "Yes, I am home," she caroled. "And yes, I had a wonderful—" She broke off, staring at her mother's tear-stained face. "Mom? Dad?" She looked at her father, who was holding and rocking her. "What's wrong?"

"Oh, Janis," her mother sobbed. "One of our babies is dead."

"Talia had pneumonia," her father said, meeting her stunned gaze. "She just couldn't take any more."

Janis fell back a step. No. Talia wasn't even *two;* she *couldn't* be dead. She didn't even have all her teeth yet.

"She never got to see her room at Harmony House," her mother said, eyes streaming. She made a fist and shaking it, stormed away from her husband. "That house has got to be opened! This *cannot* happen again! Ever! If they have to die, let them die in their own beds, surrounded by toys and people who love them." Her shoulders slumped. "Oh, Trent," she said in a small voice.

"I'm here," he said immediately, going to her.

Janis bent slowly, feeling very old. She picked up her purse and one of the cats, then made her way upstairs.

Isis purred and nuzzled her chin.

"Stay and keep me warm," Janis whispered.

Eleven

Maria stared at herself in the girls' room mirror. She had gotten to school early on purpose, wanting to test her make-up under these lights.

"Not too bad," she said, poofing out her bottom lip. A scab was forming along the gash, which made her lipstick look a little lumpy but at least the swelling had gone down.

She tilted her head, peering at the layer of foundation and plum-colored blush. "I look like I'm ready for Hallowe'en," she said but was pleased at how the blush blended with the bruise. "If I keep my hair forward, no one will ever know."

Except her.

And Leif.

She closed her eyes, blocking the wave of fury that began to break over her. She had felt this way twice yesterday, once during Sunday dinner when her mother had suggested going to the doctor to see if her lip needed stitches and the second when she'd dragged the clammy dress and shredded

153

stockings from under her bed and buried them in an outward-bound garbage bag.

"Hey there, Queenie," Vanessa drawled. "You're here early."

"You, too," Maria said, dying. Of all the people she didn't want to see, Vanessa topped the list. "What're you doing here?"

Vanessa ambled up next to her, watching Maria in the mirror. "I wanted to be the first to congratulate you for Saturday."

"You already did," Maria said, puzzled.

"I don't mean *that,* I mean on your new anniversary. Now we can finally add you to our celebration list."

"Vanessa," Maria said helplessly, "I don't know what you're talking about."

"Oh, give it a rest already, will you?" she snapped. "Why do you always have to act so innocent? Leif told us, Torres. About you and him doing the nasty in the park after the dance? Was it as good as he said or is he full of it?"

The blood drained from Maria's face. *"What?"*

Vanessa's eyebrows rose. "So he *wasn't* any good?"

"He's lying." Maria's stomach churned and sweat broke out on her forehead. "I . . . we . . . we never did that. He drove me home, that's all." The blood returned to her face, making it burn with shame.

Vanessa gave her a sly look. "That's not what I think," she said in a singsong voice. "And neither does anyone else . . ."

"What do you mean, 'anyone else?' " Maria cried.

She laughed. "Don't worry, he made you sound like some kind of Madonna erotica-equal or something. You really rocked him, Torres. Are you sure you don't want him back? I mean God, he'd probably do anything you want now—"

Black dots danced in front of Maria's eyes. It was over. If Vanessa knew, everyone knew. Everyone thought she had slept with Leif. She, Maria Torres, who had never slept with anyone.

"No, I don't want him," she said in a cold, hard voice. "*You* can have him if you want. But keep a tissue handy," she added, gathering her purse and heading for the door. "He slobbers."

"Brian." Janis tapped his shoulder.

"Hey, hi," he said, turning from his open locker and giving her a welcoming smile.

"One of our HIV-infected babies died Saturday night," she said. "Her name was Talia. She wasn't even two years old."

"Oh, no," he said and opened his arms.

Her tears came like a downpour.

"Hi, Maria," Stephanie said as Maria strode up to the locker. "I hear you're Queen. Congratulations. How was the dance?"

"Hi. Yes. Thank you. Fine." Maria's hands shook as she twisted the lock, missing the combination. She swore, kicked it, then leaned her fore-head against the cold steel.

Stephanie watched, open-mouthed.

"I'm sorry," Maria whispered. Her smile was per-fect but her eyes shone with pain. "The dance was great. Janis and Brian are now seeing each other. It was great, just great."

"Maria." Stephanie put a hand on her arm and was shocked to find her trembling. "Are you okay?"

"Hey Maria." Stan, one of the football players stopped alongside of her. "Want to meet me in the park at lunchtime? We can have a little party. Just you and me."

Stephanie's jaw dropped.

"Go away." Maria bent her head, disappearing beneath her hair and fumbled with the lock.

"Why?" he said defensively. "I'm not good enough?"

"Don't you ever talk to her like that again!" Stephanie blurted, balling her slender hands into fists and glaring up at him. "Who do you think you are, anyway?"

"The next in line," he said, laughing and saunter-ing away.

"Bonehead," Stephanie muttered. "Boy, if Frances were here, she would've ripped out his tongue."

Maria's laugh sounded suspiciously like a sob.

"You guys aren't gonna, like, hand feed each

other forever, are you?" Natalie said, grinning across the lunchtable at Janis and Brian. "I mean, Stephanie and Phillip are a couple and they're not googling at each other."

Janis drew herself up. "I," she announced loftily, handing Brian back his fork, "do not google."

"I knew that would do it," Natalie said, nudging Cassandra and interrupting her quiet conversation with Maria. "Oh, sorry. Go back to whatever you were saying."

"I'm fine," Maria said, avoiding Cassandra's concerned gaze. "I mean, Leif definitely lied when he told you he was taking me home but how were you supposed to know that?"

"I should have found you and made sure," Cassandra insisted. "The only reason I didn't was because the dance was almost over and Natalie really wanted to leave . . ." She winced at the slip.

"Don't worry about it," Maria said, toying with her chow mein. "Leif took me home and everything was fine." She dropped her fork and shoved the tray away. "I can't finish this."

"But you didn't eat anything," Cassandra said. Her gaze roamed over Maria's profile, taking in the puffy lip and the dark shadow beneath the heavy face make-up. "Want some of my yogurt?"

"No, I'm not really hungry," Maria mumbled, brushing her hair forward to cover her cheek.

Cassandra glanced around the table, wondering if anyone else had noticed the change in Maria.

157

She met Stephanie's worried gaze, hoping for answers, but Stephanie only shrugged.

Janis bopped down the hall to ceramics class. Even though a part of her mourned Talia, another part, the part that pushed her forward into life, was humming like a high-tension wire. She had so much to do and not enough time to do it. Thanksgiving was only days away and right after that, Fur-Free Friday. She had posters to make, people to contact, baskets of food for the needy to pack and absolutely no time to see Brian.

"We can hardly say 'hi,' before it's time for his football practice or for me to rush down to the hospital to rock the babies," she said, running a finger up and down her spiral notebook, enjoying the sound. "I've been seeing Brian for three whole days and that's about all we've been able to do. *See* each other. I don't know any more about him now than I did before—"

"Talking to yourself, Veg-Head?"

Janis glanced over and found Connie, Frank Geery's skinhead girlfriend, cruising along beside her like a camouflaged tank. "Very good," she applauded mockingly. "I've been telling all your teachers you can form sentences but they wouldn't believe me."

The insult passed right over Connie's shorn head. "You like that Oreo?" she asked, shoving her hands deep into her fatigues.

"Huh?" Janis said, confused.

"That Oreo," Connie said impatiently. "You know, the L. A. mutt—half-black, half-white?"

"Get away from me," Janis blurted, aghast. "I thought Frank was the most ignorant person in Chandler but I see now that he's got competition."

"That doesn't mean anything to me," Connie said, shrugging.

"I rest my case," Janis said grimly and sailed ahead of Connie into ceramics.

"Oh, Cassandra, that's great!" Janis cried, clapping and giving an excited hop. "What made you decide to march with us?"

Cassandra thought a moment. "Meeting Star. I mean, I never really realized fur came from live animals until I met Star and ever since then, I haven't been able to forget."

"It's a kicker, isn't it, when you start seeing things for what they really are? So, how do you want to do this?"

"Can you give me the details now?" Cassandra asked, glancing at her watch. It was Wednesday, the day before Thanksgiving and because they were getting out early, her next class was in less than three minutes. It would have been easier just to call Janis at home and discuss it but that was out of the question. If her parents discovered she was doing something as 'flaky' as attending an animal rights rally, they'd ground her for life.

"Sure," Janis said easily. "It starts Friday at noon at RBK Furriers up on the highway. Don't

159

park in their lot or you may get towed. Wear something warm, no fur, no leather. Don't worry about a sign, we bring extras."

Cassandra hesitated, twisting her pearl ring. "Are we going to get in trouble, Janis?"

"You mean arrested? No. This is a peaceful demonstration. Oh yeah, one more thing. If anybody from the fur store tries to take your picture, look the other way. According to the scoop, they're trying to assemble some kind of nationwide catalogue of animal rights 'terrorists' or something." She grinned, not looking in the least disturbed. "I'll see you on Friday. Rain or shine."

"Have a good Thanksgiving, Janis. Turkey-free?"

"Bet on it," Janis said, raising a triumphant fist.

Cassandra headed for class. A nationwide terrorist catalogue? she thought in dismay. But I'm a *ballerina*.

"I love getting out of school early," Natalie said, facing Cassandra and walking backwards across the parking lot. "It makes me feel like I'm getting away with something."

"You won't be if you trip over that curb," Cassandra said.

"Don't you ever do anything strange, Cass, just to see if you're capable?" Natalie said, sighing and facing the right way. "Like—" She broke off, eyes wide. "Oh no, don't look now but who's sitting in that black van parked in the same row as us?"

160

"How am I supposed to tell if I'm not allowed to look?"

"Be creative," Natalie snapped. "Pretend you're watching a plane or something. Hurry."

"A plane," Cassandra said, frowning up into the empty sky. "Okay." She glanced at the van. "Edan Parrish and he's not in the van anymore, Natalie. He's coming this way. Hi, Edan."

"Hi, Cassandra." His amber gaze shifted. "Hello, Natalie."

"Hello," Natalie said, folding her arms across her chest. "What're you doing here?"

"Natalie," Cassandra said, frowning.

"That's okay," Edan said with a smile. "I'm used to it. Listen, would you mind if I talked to Natalie for a minute?"

"Of course not," Cassandra said. "I'll wait in the car."

"Well?" Natalie set her chin, trying to ignore the softness in his eyes. It was impossible. Just being near him, not even touching, made her skin tingle. A strand of hair drifted across his cheek and she found herself wanting to stroke it away.

"Hi, tiger," he said quietly. "I missed you."

She had no words to give back so she stayed still as his gaze searched hers, letting him pierce her cactuslike defenses and see into the most battered, vulnerable corner of her heart.

"That's what I needed to know," he said and cupping her face between his strong, calloused hands, bent and kissed her. His lips were slow and sweet, his touch powerfully gentle.

161

No one had ever kissed her like this or caressed her face. No one had ever pressed her hand to his heart, letting her feel its ragged beat or held her with such tenderness.

But Edan did, here in the middle of the crowded school parking lot, with his eyes glowing like the sun and the brisk, November wind rippling through his hair.

"You're driving me crazy, you know," he said huskily.

"Oh, yeah?" she said, feeling bizarrely shy. "Well, it's a rough job but somebody's gotta do it."

"Uh . . . guys?" Cassandra stood next to them, eyes averted and lips twitching. "I hate to break up your . . . uh, *conversation—*"

"Isn't she subtle?" Natalie said wryly.

"—but I have an early ballet practice today and I really do have to get going." Her smile turned mischievous. "Gee, I hope I draw as big an audience at my dance competition as you did in this parking lot. I don't know, maybe I'm in the wrong business. Mouth-to-mouth resuscitation looks like a lot more fun."

"That does it!" Natalie said and took off after her fleeing, giggling cousin. "Happy Thanksgiving, Edan," she called back over her shoulder and was floored to find him right behind her.

"You didn't think I'd let you get away that easy, did you?" he said, grinning and brushing the hair from his eyes. "I want your vital stats, lady. Name, address, and phone number."

"Want to frisk me, too?" Natalie drawled and

162

collapsed against the car laughing at the shocked expressions on his and Cassandra's faces.

Some parts of life were so good.

Twelve

"Mmm, Happy Thanksgiving," Janis said, following her nose down into the kitchen. She'd slept late, had a wonderfully muzzy dream about Brian, and was still as warm as toast from sleeping amongst a litter of furry bodies. "What do I smell?"

"Wishful thinking," her mother said, smiling. She was sipping a cup of tea and reading the paper. "What you *will* soon smell is mushroom rissoles with cashew gravy, chestnut stuffing, sweet potatoes, artichoke hearts pickled in garlic and vinegar, and fresh biscuits."

"My stomach can't wait. Where's Daddy?" Janis said, padding to the fridge and pouring herself a glass of fresh apple juice.

"Delivering more holiday food boxes," Mrs. Sandifer-Wayne said. "The church called with two more shut-ins no one had added to their list and asked if we had anything extra."

"But we didn't," Janis said. "I packed and delivered all those boxes yesterday. Took me until after eight, remember? And I don't think the food bank is open today."

"We managed."

"Ah. An all night grocery store or our own pantry?"

"Both," her mother said with a satisfied smile.

"Not the everyday dishes, Natalie. Cassandra," Aunt Miriam's voice was smooth but impatient, "please show Natalie how to set the table."

"What's so hard about setting a table?" Natalie muttered, following her cousin back into the elegant dining room.

"We use the good china on the holidays. And don't drop them," she added, handing Natalie the first delicate, gold-rimmed plate from the cabinet. "This is their wedding china."

Natalie crept across the room, holding the single plate in front of her like an offering to the gods. Bowing, she set it on the damask tablecloth, folded a matching cloth napkin at its left and placed the ornate, polished silverware nearby.

"Very nice," Aunt Miriam said, watching from the doorway. "But tuck the ends of the napkin under. It's sloppy otherwise."

Sighing, Natalie did as she was told. The table was magnificent and the heady scent of roasting turkey was whipping her taste buds into a frenzy. Everything was magazine-perfect . . .

Not like last Thanksgiving, when her mother

had had to work. Elizabeth Bell hadn't had time to make a turkey and Natalie hadn't been willing, so they'd called a temporary truce and met at McDonald's, sharing Big Macs and fries in the front seat of the patrol car.

I wonder if her and that dumb dog Locust are having turkey, Natalie thought, placing a crystal wine glass above the plate and watching as Aunt Miriam adjusted its position.

"That's better," her aunt said, beaming. "Now go and get the next plate please, Natalie."

She did, but in her mind she was opening a grease-stained bag and slipping her fingers past the food shells, tweezing up the stray fries littering the bottom of the sack. And no matter how many there were, Natalie thought, my mother always let me eat every one of them. Why didn't she ever ask me to share? I would have given her some if she'd asked me.

"Fold the napkin under, Natalie," her aunt reminded her.

The only reason nobody questioned Maria's strange behavior at dinner and then afterward, when she curled up on the couch under an afghan, watching and listening but not contributing, was because she lied and told her mother she had cramps. The message, never spoken aloud, was passed on with a raised eyebrow or meaningful look, explaining the unmentionable to her father, Jesse, and her grandparents.

"Would you like a heating pad?" her grandmother Torres offered, bending over Maria's huddled figure.

"Or a nice glass of warm milk?" her grandmother Cimarron murmured, stroking the hair back from Maria's forehead.

"How about an aspirin?" her mother said.

They sat with her, forming a protective, unpenetrable circle, shooing Jesse off when his teasing angered her and scolding her father when his pride at her being Homecoming Queen made her cry.

"This turkey's dry," Anastasia said, throwing down her lipstick-stained fork. "I'm not eating dry turkey."

"Well if you had basted it when I told you to, it wouldn't be dry," Stephanie said, struggling to keep her voice even.

"Now Stephanie," her mother said nervously. "You know Ana had some very important errands to run this morning."

"What kind of errands could a thirteen-year-old girl have on Thanksgiving Day?" Stephanie asked, eyeing her sister.

"None of your business," Anastasia said sullenly.

"I think the turkey's dee-licious," Corinne said, smiling at Stephanie and shoveling another piece into her mouth.

"Thank you." She glanced at Phillip, who shot her a silly smile. "Is it really that dry?"

His smile widened. "Water," he gasped, clutching his throat.

"Told you," Ana said triumphantly.

Stephanie's stomach hurt. "If it's that bad, don't eat it."

"Good." Anastasia shoved back her chair. "Take me for a ride on your Harley, Phillip."

"No," Stephanie said without giving him a chance to respond. "You have to help clean up." And besides, Phillip was way too stoned to even stay on the road.

"Mom," Anastasia whirled on her mother.

"Well," her mother's hands fluttered like agitated birds. "I don't see what's wrong with a five-minute ride." She avoided Stephanie's eyes. "Corinne will help you clean up."

"Sure, Steph," Phillip said, scrambling out of his chair like he was glad to escape. "We'll be back in five."

"Or ten," Ana called over her shoulder, following him out.

"I'm going to lay down for a while," Mrs. Ling said, flitting into the living room.

"I'll stay with you, Steph," Corinne said.

"No, you've done more than your share," Stephanie said, forcing a smile. "You go play." She watched her sister leave the table, then grimly speared another slab of turkey. "Happy Thanksgiving," she said, to no one.

Thirteen

"Yes," Janis called, raising a triumphant fist as a car beeped in support of the demonstrators. The day had been perfect; no more than a quick sprinkle at noon, a much larger turn-out than expected, and a staggering assortment of anti-fur signs, most sporting graphic photos of the agony behind the coat. The furrier's business seemed to be down today, too.

" 'Every fur coat hurts!' " Cassandra chanted, lifting her sign over her head. Her eyes were sparkling and her cheeks flushed. "Do you really think all the people who've beeped mean they're against killing animals for fur coats?"

Janis shrugged, not wanting to burst her bubble. "Every time we go public, more people realize that slaughtering and skinning animals isn't something to be proud of."

"You should've brought Star," Cassandra said. "She's living proof of the brutality of steel-jaw traps."

"She's in her hibernation mode right now. She made a nest under the back porch—"

"Outside? Alone?" Cassandra looked worried. "Aren't you afraid she'll run away or something?"

"Cassandra, she's free to go anytime," Janis said, sighing. "We only share our home with her, we can't make her stay." Her eyes lit up. "Brian!" she shouted, waving. "Over here! Oh my God, this is great!"

"Chandler News," a reporter said. "Can I ask what you hope to accomplish today?"

"Cassandra will help you," she said as Brian strode towards her. His cheeks were ruddy, his hair tousled by the wind, and suddenly, she realized how much she had missed him. "She's new to animal rights and can give you a fresh perspective."

"Janis," Brian said, weaving through the demonstrators.

"Hi," she said, meeting him halfway.

"What're you doing?" he asked grimly.

"We're demonstrating, what does it look like we're doing?" She spread her hands, nearly smacking him with her sign.

"No, this," he said, pointing at the photo of an emaciated coyote cowering in a trap. "How could you spread this crap?"

Janis's jaw dropped. "This isn't crap, this is how fur coats are made, by killing innocent animals." Every word seemed to make his face more thunderous. "Brian, what's wrong with you?" A car horn beeped and automatically, Janis raised her fist. "Every fur coat hurts!" she chanted. "Say no to fur!"

He grabbed her arm. "Stop. Please Janis, go

170

home."

"Why?"

"Because I'm asking you to."

"I want a reason," she said stubbornly.

"Because RBK Furriers is my father," he said defiantly.

"What?" She fell back a step, reeling.

"I work here," he continued. "It's my family's business."

She stared at him, horrified. "You sell slaughtered animals? You sell murdered coyotes and raccoons and minks and bobcats—"

"Janis—"

"No," she cried in revulsion. "Don't touch me."

"Cut it out," he said stiffly.

"How many coyotes does it take to make one coat, Brian, if you only use the soft, belly fur from each animal?" she said, overcome with fury. "How many fox are anally electrocuted, how many mink get their necks snapped, how many 'trash' animals do your suppliers cripple in their traps, how many eagles or cats or dogs or deer die in agony so some vain, self-centered woman can wrap herself in carcasses and pretend she's important?"

"You make it sound like I'm killing those animals *myself,*" he said angrily. "It's a business, Janis."

"And that makes it right?" She was near tears. "My God, what you know about honor I could scrape off the bottom of my *shoe.*"

He stared at her, his eyes dark with hurt. "That was low."

171

"Not as low as being a killer," she shot back raggedly. "Go away, Brian. I can't even stand to look at you right now."

"Then it's mutual," he said.

Cassandra listened to this exchange in growing horror. She'd tried distracting the reporter when it had started but he hadn't budged. Now, as Janis and Brian squared off, she moved to block his camera but was too slow. The flash went off, temporarily blinding her and she stumbled against Brian, clutching his arm for support.

The camera flashed again.

"You, too, Cassandra?" Brian sneered and strode away.

"Peaceful demonstration, huh?" the reporter said smugly.

"You did these braids yourself, didn't you girl?" the hairdresser said, meeting Natalie's gaze in the salon mirror. Lips twitching, she grabbed a handful of the lumpy, crooked braids and started unwinding them. "Lord, what a mess. Sit back and relax honey, you're gonna be here for a while."

Natalie smiled, listening with half an ear as the woman chattered and her fingers flew.

"—and so I told that man, I said, 'Baby I'm not dumb, I know where you been and I know what you been doin',' and then he started swearin' to God he hadn't been out with her but child," the hairdresser said, rolling her eyes, "he was so busy tellin' me he hadn't done me wrong that he up and

172

called me by *her* name. Now I tell you, that man had been *cheating*."

"Who?" Natalie said absently.

"My husband," she said.

"What did you do?" Natalie asked, watching the woman in the mirror. "When he called you her name, I mean."

"Threw his trumpet out the window," the woman said, laughing so hard she had to stop unbraiding. "And he almost went with it."

"Whoa," Natalie said, torn between admiration and a dark, creeping sense of uneasiness. "So, you're divorcing him?"

"Now why would I do that?" She snorted and resumed her work. "He's a musician, child. It wasn't the first time and as long as there are women out there who love jazz, it won't be the last."

Natalie's hands were cold. "Then why do you stay with him?"

The hairdresser looked surprised. "Because he's a good man. I love him. He loves his babies and he's always there for me."

Except when he's out cheating, Natalie thought.

"Don't tell me you've never been cheated on," the woman said, catching Natalie's skeptical look.

"I've been cheated on," Natalie replied shortly.

"And what did you do about it?"

"Dumped them."

"What about now? Are you with anybody now?"

"Sort of." She didn't really want to talk about Edan. The relationship, what there was of it, was still too new to be dissected like some poor, biology

173

lab frog.

"Well, how do you know what he's doing right now?" the woman said, planting her hands on her hips.

"I don't," Natalie said. The chill was creeping higher, like a slow, steady case of frostbite.

"But you love him, so you just have to trust him to do right by you." Satisfied, the woman stepped back and fluffed Natalie's spirals. "Now let's do your hair. You in school, baby?"

"Seven Pines," Natalie said, staring at her reflection.

Did she love Edan?

She wanted him. Was that the same thing?

Did she trust him?

She watched her face change, watched as her jaw rose and her eyes narrowed. Did she trust him?

No.

Stephanie stood outside The Green Café, shifting from foot to foot and shivering. She had gotten off work twenty minutes ago and Phillip still wasn't here to pick her up. She could have waited for him inside but she was tired of pretending to laugh at the waitress's cracks about Phillip's undependability.

"Come on," she muttered, blowing on her red, chapped hands. Her gray wool gloves had finally fallen apart but in one more day, she'd be able to sort through the Café's Lost and Found box and find a new pair of unclaimed ones.

Phillip's motorcycle roared around the corner and stopped at the curb. Grinning, Phillip slid forward, motioning her onto the seat behind him. "Sorry I'm late but I had to see Jared."

It was the last straw. "Of course you did," she snapped, jamming her helmet over her head and climbing onto the Harley.

"What's with you?" he said, startled.

"I'm tired and I'm freezing, okay?"

"Okay." He revved the bike and peeled away from the curb. "I said I was sorry," he shouted back over his shoulder.

"Well, sorry's just not cutting it tonight," she muttered, knowing he couldn't hear her. She was still annoyed at him for keeping Ana out for fifteen minutes yesterday and for mocking on her turkey dinner. She'd gotten up early on her day off to cook that food, knowing that with his parents away chasing royalty on St. Kitts he wouldn't have any holiday at all.

"Let's go to my house, Steph, and I'll make it up to you."

She shrugged. "Fine."

Janis ripped the page from her pad, crumpled it up, and threw it over her shoulder. The cats tensed, tails lashing, and pounced, batting the paper around her bedroom.

"Do you have to do that now? Can't you see I've got Letters to the Editors to write?" The purpose of her mission returned and with a groan, she

175

dropped her head into her hands. "How could I have been so stupid? He's a *furrier,* someone who deals in death for profit! I can't believe it. How could he be so gentle with me and then promote the cruelest business in the world?" Her eyes filled with tears. "I was so happy to see him, too . . ."

She sat for a moment, sunk in misery, then her gaze fell on the stack of anti-fur posters and literature she'd gathered up and her temper began to burn. He had kissed her and made her believe he was everything she'd ever dreamed about . . . and then in one brutal move, shattered the ideal into a million pieces.

" 'Dear Editor,' " she began, writing furiously. " 'For those who believe the fur industry's myth that wearing animal skins is classy, I'd like to explain what happens between the time the animal is alive and minding its own business to the time its skin ends up hanging on a rack in a store like RBK Furriers.' "

She finished the eighth letter after midnight and laid it carefully on the posters she would nail up around town on Sunday.

Maybe Brian's like everyone else, maybe he just never realized the truth behind the furs, she thought without any real hope. Maybe once he understands what really happens . . .

"Face it," she said, blinking back tears. "It's over."

Stephanie sat at the end of the couch, fuming.

They had no sooner gotten to Phillip's than he'd left her in the kitchen making coffee and disappeared into his room.

And I know what he's doing in there, too, she thought, stirring her coffee. Jared plus picking me up late equals coke.

"Hey, Stephie, miss me?" Phillip said, plopping down next to her and slinging an arm across her legs.

The momentum sent coffee sloshing out of the cup and onto her pink sweater. "Oh no! Now it's ruined." She shoved his arm away and slammed the cup down on the table.

"No sweat," he drawled. "It's an old one, right? I mean, you've worn it a hundred times."

"But it's the only pink one I have," she cried, hurt by his amused tone. "You wouldn't think it was so funny if I ruined your leather jacket."

He shrugged. "Go ahead. I'll just get another one."

"Just forget it," she said, near tears.

"Hey, c'mon I didn't do it on purpose. I wouldn't hurt you Steph, I love you." He eased her down on the couch next to him. "We haven't been together in so long." He nuzzled her neck.

"Can I ask you something?" she said, stopping him. "Is it hard for you to be with me when you're not high? I mean, when we started going out you were hardly ever high and now every single time I see you, you're stoned."

"You keeping track?" he said, sitting up. "My parents aren't worried, so why should you be?"

"Phillip, your parents aren't around enough to even know you're getting high, so how can they worry?"

"Good point," he said sarcastically. He glanced back down at her and his gaze softened. "You know the way I am. Getting high for me is a good time. I don't ask you to get high, so why should it bother you if I do?"

She struggled with that for a moment. It sounded logical on the surface but there was more to it. "Because it makes me feel like us being together isn't enough to make you happy anymore."

"*Now* you're imagining things," he said, stretching back out next to her. "The only time I *am* happy is when I'm with you. The rest of the time I'm just . . . passing time."

"Really?" She searched his face, ran her fingers across his firm, stubbled chin and cheeks.

"I can prove it," he said, grinning. "Take next Saturday night off work and I'll throw you the best seventeenth birthday party this town's ever seen."

She caught her breath. "No, really? I mean, you said you might but I never . . . can I invite Janis and Natalie and them?"

"You can invite the whole school if you want."

"Wow," she whispered, envisioning it. "I've never had a serious birthday party before." She gazed up at him, her eyes dark with wonder. "You would go through all that for me?"

"Sure," he said, tracing her mouth with his fingertip. "Look at what you go through for me every single day. I love you."

"Show me," she murmured.

"Well, cross the mall off the list," Maria muttered, striding into her room and slamming the door. She had made the incredibly stupid mistake of going shopping on a Saturday night and had suffered the consequences.

Leif, Stan, and a load of other football players had been hanging out by the arcade. She had rounded the corner and walked right into them. And then when she'd tried to leave . . .

"Back for more?" Leif had said, hitching his thumbs in his pockets and tilting his head back.

"Nah, she's here for me," Stan said, sliding an arm around her rigid shoulders. "Gimme the keys to your Tranny, Leif."

"Let go," Maria said, gritting her teeth. She shoved Stan's arm away, turned, and was body-blocked by Leif. She froze, staring into his eyes, scared and shaking and mortified, and suddenly, the roaring, red rage that was now as much a part of her as her name turned to bone-chilling hate. If she was a slut, then they were the ones who had made her that way, with their groping hands and expectant eyes and rotten, cowardly lies.

"C'mon." Leif grabbed her arm. "Let's go another round."

"No way," she heard herself snap, sounding remarkably like Vanessa. "It was so boring I fell asleep the first time."

Leif turned scarlet and released her like she was

on fire. The rest of the guys hooted and howled with laughter.

"And that drooling," she continued in a cold, disdainful voice. "Really, Leif. If you don't find a way to control your slobber, nobody's ever gonna go out with you again." Her smile sliced through his feeble blustering. "Don't worry, I'm not even gonna go into that other stuff about your 900 number phone friend and all." She glanced at her watch. "Well, gotta go. See you."

Maria had held her breath until she rounded the corner, then sagged against the wall.

Now there was no going back . . .

Nope, none, Maria thought grimly, kicking off her boots. If she was a tease, then so be it but if Leif thought he had power over her now, he was sorely mistaken. She might not have been able to fight him physically (and that memory burned like a cancer, spreading through her body and eating away at her heart) but hanging with Vanessa had taught her how to fight dirty, how to find somebody's weak spot and tear into it like a pit bull.

"And I'm his weak spot," she said, feeling sick. "Maria the tease. Well, he ain't seen nothin' yet."

Cassandra practiced her competition solo for two hours on Sunday morning, then tripped lightly down to breakfast. "Good morn—" She broke off at her parents' stony gazes. "What's wrong?"

Her father shoved the morning paper across the table at her.

180

Cassandra stared at the photo on the front page. 'PEACEFUL PROTEST GONE SOUR' the headline screamed and underneath it was a picture of her, Janis, and Brian in front of RBK Furriers. "Oh, no," she breathed, sinking into a chair. The photo had caught her when she'd stumbled and grabbed his arm, making it look like she was holding him while Janis hit him. "That stupid reporter."

"What were you doing there?" her father said in an ominously quiet voice. "What was my daughter doing brawling in public?"

"That's not what happened," she said, scanning the article. Although the picture was awful, the text was fairly sympathetic, quoting Janis's impassioned speech and listing the variety of animals RBK Furriers sold as coats. "I —"

"Humiliated our family," her mother said, rising and pacing the kitchen. "Really Cassandra, Chelsea never embarrassed us this way and even Carlton, as young as he is, has never done anything so . . . so . . . *unfixable*. Not even Natalie has been so thoughtless."

"You are grounded," her father said. "School, ballet, home."

"For how long?" she said, knowing better than to argue.

"That will depend on you," he said.

"One hundred," Janis said, hammering in the last nail. Wearily, she stepped back and eyed the poster hanging on the pole in front of RBK Furri-

181

ers. It was less gruesome than the ones with photos but the facts were still horrible. Thousands of animals.

"Read this, Brian," she muttered. "And then try to defend your business."

The phone rang while Natalie and Cassandra were watching TV.

"You get it," Natalie said. "If it's for me, I'm not here."

Cassandra's hand hovered over the receiver. "What if it's Edan?"

She shrugged, avoiding her cousin's gaze. "I'm not here."

"Natalie—"

"Cass, please get it before your mother does," Natalie said.

"You know I'm a bad liar," she said, scowling and answering the phone. "Hello?"

"Hi, Cassandra," Edan said cheerfully. "Is your beautiful, bratty cousin around?"

"Uh, hi Edan," Cassandra said brightly, glaring at Natalie. "My cousin? Natalie? Uh no, she's not . . . um, here."

"Oh no? Where'd she go?"

"Um . . . I don't know."

"Oh." Silence. "Any idea when she'll be back?"

"Uh . . . no." She wanted to kill Natalie.

"She's there, isn't she?" he said, sounding quietly hurt.

Darn you, Natalie, she thought.

"So she doesn't want to talk to me." He sighed. "Okay Cass, just tell her if she wants me, I'll be around. Bye."

"Bye." She hung up and turned to face Natalie. "He knew."

Natalie looked down and didn't reply.

Fourteen

"So, the party's gonna be this Saturday night at Phillip's and everyone's invited," Stephanie burbled, beaming around the lunchtable. "Maria, tell your brother and the rest of the band too, okay? Not to play, just to have fun."

"They usually have a gig on Saturday night," Maria said, cracking her gum. "But sure, I'll pass it on. No problem."

Stephanie stared at her, frowning, then at the rest of her new friends' faces. Something was different today and it wasn't a good kind of 'different.' Maria was sitting backwards on her chair, chin propped on her fist and snapping her gum. And her black catsuit was . . . well, more like something Natalie would wear.

And Natalie . . . she was a walking thundercloud, silent and threatening. Cassandra, usually picture-perfect, had wisps of hair escaping from her bun and a thread hanging from her cuff. And she was chewing on her fingernails. Janis's smile was grimly cheerful and her eyes way too bright, like she was holding back tears. And Brian was sitting with the football players.

"What the heck is going on here?" Stephanie blurted. "I mean, I thought you guys would be happy . . ."

"We are," Janis said, wincing as loud laughter came from the jock's table. "And we'll definitely be there, won't we?"

Everyone nodded and Stephanie had to be satisfied with that.

Natalie and Cassandra walked silently to the car after school. Cassandra still hadn't forgiven her cousin for making her lie to Edan and Natalie's stubborn refusal to discuss it only aggravated her further.

Everything's falling apart, Cassandra thought. I'm grounded, my parents are mad, people have been calling the house and hanging up and they're blaming it on my activism—

"Wait," Natalie said suddenly, staring at the macadam around the BMW. Her lips tightened and her hands clenched into fists.

Cassandra followed her gaze. "What the heck . . . ?" she said wonderingly, staring at all the Oreo cookies scattered around her car. "Did somebody drop a grocery bag or something?"

Natalie's laugh was harsh. "No, this is meant for me. The skinheads don't like the fact that Edan kiss . . . talked to me."

"But why?"

"It's an insult, Cass. Half-black, half-white, get it?"

185

"Then we should report this," Cassandra said angrily, stepping around the cookies to unlock her door. "Oh, my God!"

"What?" Natalie flew to her side.

"My poor car," Cassandra moaned, crouching and running her fingers along a deep, fresh scratch that ran from fender to fender. "Why would they do this?"

"You're my cousin," Natalie said flatly. "That's enough."

"They can't get away with it," she said, staring pleadingly up at Natalie. "We'll report them—"

"Time to join the real world, Cass," Natalie said, snorting. "They already did get away with it. You see any witnesses?"

"There might be somebody . . ." Cassandra stopped at the look in Natalie's eyes. "There won't be, will there?"

"Now you're learning," Natalie said. "Come on, show's over. We gave them enough to laugh about today."

Cassandra rose, zombielike, and they drove away in silence.

Maria sauntered down the hallway, nibbling on an apple. Her pants were so tight she could hardly breathe and her shirt so low-cut she couldn't bend over without risking total exposure. She felt cheap and ugly and hard, exactly what they'd branded her.

Stan and Leif were heading down the hall. They were acting up and hadn't noticed her yet.

Please God, she prayed silently, let them go right by. Don't let them stop and—

"Hey, baby," Stan said, body blocking her. "Lookin' for me?"

"Sure," she said, glancing at Leif, who was staring at her like a penniless kid at the candy counter. Ignoring him, she smiled at Stan and nibbled the apple. "Want a bite?"

"No," he said.

"How about of the apple?" she drawled, arching an eyebrow.

"Hey, I want to change my answer," he protested, laughing.

"Too late," she said, shrugging. "Bye, Stan." She glanced at Leif, sniffed, and walked away. He'd looked about ready to cry.

What a shame.

"What's wrong with you, Cassandra?" Miss Tatiana asked, frowning. "Your legs are shaky, your pirouettes are, at best, those of an amateur and you move like a wooden toy. Where is the joy, the longing, the grace? Where is your control?"

Cassandra flushed. "I'm sorry. I'll keep practicing."

"You must. The competition is this Sunday and you're my prize student." She patted Cassandra's abdomen. "And suck this in. It's small but noticeable. No desserts for you this week."

I'm losing it, Cassandra thought despairingly, then gritted her teeth. No, I'm not. I *won't*. I'm the only Taylor without a trophy on our mantelpiece and I'm going to win. This is what I'm good at; all I have to do is put my mind to it.

She lifted her chin and began to dance.

* * *

Janis grabbed the stack of newspapers from the front seat of the Bronco and headed for the house.

"Every single one of them," she marveled, taking the steps two at a time. "That must be some kind of record. Eight Letters to the Editors about animal rights on the same day. Wow."

She was struggling to grasp the doorknob when she heard a car pulling into the driveway behind her.

"Janis?"

"Dad?" she said, going still. "What're you doing home?"

"Your mother called and told me to get home immediately," he said, flinging open the door. "Zoe, what's . . ." He stopped. "Zoe?"

Janis elbowed her way inside. "Mom?"

Her mother was sitting on the floor, clutching a sheet of paper. She looked up slowly, eyes shining and held it out to them. "We got it," she whispered, clasping her hands to her heart. "We've got the funding for Harmony House."

"No," her father said.

"Yes," she said, nodding. "It's all here, *in writing.*"

He whooped and seized the letter. " 'We would consider it an honor to participate in such a fine, humanitarian cause and based on your estimated operating cost, will fund the first year . . .' "

"Who? Who's doing it?" Janis said excitedly. "The church?"

Her father scanned the letter. "Robert Kelly, RBK Furriers."

The newspapers crashed to the ground.

Fifteen

Janis grabbed the letter from her father and stared at it, unable to believe it, and yet it was there, RBK Furriers. "Doesn't that just figure?" she said, shaking her head. "We've been dying for money and when it finally comes in, we can't take it." She looked up, meeting her parents puzzled faces and felt her stomach lurch. "We're not taking this, Mom. Right?"

Her mother just looked at her.

"Dad?" Janis's voice rose. She stepped backwards, away from him, away from the truth she saw in his eyes.

"Jan," her mother said softly. "We can open Harmony House."

Janis clutched the doorframe, swaying. This couldn't be happening. What about honor and principle? What about the sick, betrayed feeling cracking her heart in two? "You're selling out."

Her parents exchanged dismayed looks.

"Janis, we understand how you feel—" her father began.

"No, you don't," Janis cried. "How can you even *think* about accepting this . . . this blood money? That's what it is, you know. Filthy blood money that this guy's giving you so instead of being known as an animal-killer he's known as a 'fine humanitarian.' " Her voice broke. "All those stories you told about when you were young and everybody believed in peace, love, and changing the world were garbage, weren't they?"

"Janis—"

"But I *believed you*," Janis said, crying. "I believed you when you said 'Take a stand' or 'Protest.' I believed in daisies and Haight-Ashbury and I'm the fool who went around wearing your old clothes and listening to your old music. How could you?" She turned to run but her mother caught her arm.

"I'm sorry, sweetie," she said, holding Janis's stiff, unyielding body. "I know it must seem like a sell-out to you—"

"Don't try to justify it," Janis cried, wrenching free. "You were the ones who taught me that an excuse is an excuse and it doesn't make something right!"

"And that's still true—"

"Then how can you even *think* about using that money when you know where it came from?" She felt like she was going to throw up. "You wouldn't take that money if this was the 60s."

"You're right," her mother said, sighing heavily and sinking down into a chair. "But back in the 60s there was no such thing as AIDS and I didn't have to watch these babies dying."

"Of course not," Janis said sarcastically, lost in a swirl of temper. "Back in the 60s, you were making love, not war. Everybody was laid back and all you needed was love, right?"

"No," her mother mumbled, seeming to curl into herself. "I'm sorry if that's how I presented it to you."

"It is," Janis said, steaming.

"It was such an idealistic time," her mother said, focusing on her lap. "Everything was either black or white, there was no room for gray areas. If you weren't with us, you were against us." She raised her head, her eyes bleak. "I never told you about the time I met a Vietnam veteran in the airport, did I? He had just come home and was on crutches . . ." Her voice hitched. "He was with his mother and she was crying and I . . . I . . . I walked up and told her I would cry too if my son was a baby-killer."

"Zoe." Mr. Sandifer-Wayne started towards her.

"No," she said, meeting Janis's stunned gaze. "I want to tell her the truth, Trent. I want her to know how that poor mother's face crumpled and how I was so stupidly smug. Protesting the war was far more important than one boy's homecoming and that will haunt me until I die." She wiped her cheeks. "There's no excuse for the way I acted Janis, but there are *reasons* and the reason we're going to accept this donation is those children."

Janis stared at her.

"It's not all black and white anymore," her

mother said.

"That's easy to say." Janis turned and went up to her room.

"Maria?" Mr. Garcia's voice stopped her on the way out the door. "Can you stay after class a moment?"

Maria hesitated, then sighed. "Sure."

Several guys nudged each other and grinning, left the room.

"What was that all about?" Mr. Garcia said, eyeing their retreating figures.

Maria shrugged. "They're just a bunch of jerks. What did you want to see me about?" She toyed with laces on the front of her shirt, avoiding his surprised look.

"Nothing important," he said after a moment. "I was just wondering how Homecoming went. The Leif situation, I mean."

"Oh." She pretended to examine her nail polish, knowing that if she met his warm, uncondemning gaze, she would burst into tears. "It went great, just great."

"He didn't give you any trouble?"

She didn't know what hurt worse; the concern in his voice or the lies she had to tell him. "Nope, not a thing."

"Maria, look at me," he said quietly.

"Can't," she said, panicking. "Gotta go. See you."

* * *

"Hey, Cass, how did you get ungrounded in time to get Stephanie a birthday present?" Natalie said, closing her locker.

"I said I realized the demonstration was an irresponsible act that could have affected my future," Cassandra said, sighing. "I just said what they wanted to hear so I could get out. I don't know what's going on anymore. Between the grounding and those hang-up calls and the skinheads, it's like nothing's going right. My ballet's suffering, the competition's the Sunday after Stephanie's party, and—"

"What did you get her?" Natalie interrupted.

"A lockable journal. Maria said she likes to write."

"I got her a teal bodysuit. It'll look great with her hair."

"That's nice," Cassandra said, swallowing her annoyance at being cut off. "Maria got her a pair of earrings and a bracelet."

"Janis and Simon went in on a pair of hand-knit mittens and a scarf from some Third World country that sells through UNICEF," Natalie said, grinning. "Leave it to Janis to help the world."

"I wish there was a way we could help her and Brian." Cassandra shot her cousin a weighty look. "But I guess everyone has to work out their own relationships, huh?"

Natalie didn't answer.

If nothing is cut and dry anymore, Janis thought,

trudging down the hall, then how am I supposed to know what's right? I mean, if the line between the good guys and bad guys falls, how am I supposed to know who I am? Brian's father sells coats made from dead, fur-bearing animals. This is wrong. My parents are taking his money to fund Harmony House. Isn't that wrong, too?

"This is giving me a pain," Janis groaned, walking up beside Simon and resting her forehead on his shoulder. "Help me, Simon. Bore a hole in my brain and let the sap run out. I can't deal with this anymore."

"Deal with what?" he said, tousling her hair.

"Quit it. You know I hate that," she said, scowling.

"Now that's more like it," he said. "A whining Janis is a pesty Janis. If you miss Brian that much, why don't you just get back with him instead of torturing the rest of us?"

"Because I'm not talking about Brian, I'm talking about . . ." She hesitated, feeling disloyal. "Oh, never mind. I'll figure it out myself."

"Ah, sweet mystery of life," he drawled, grinning.

She shot him an annoyed look and left. Simon was fun most of the time but when she was serious, he got on her nerves. "If I'd have told him about the funding, he probably would have said, 'Who cares where it comes from, Janni? Just do good with it now,' but that would be like using drug money to fund a clinic. It doesn't balance . . ." She stopped walking. "Or does it? Yes, the money is tainted and

194

it shouldn't be accepted," she said slowly, wandering into the stairwell. "But if it has to go somewhere, shouldn't it help people instead of being put back into the fur business, which would only cause *more* suffering? Is that the balance?"

Absently, she opened the door to the lower hallway. "So if a donation from social services would've been considered white and a donation from a slaughterhouse black, then a donation from a furrier to house abandoned children would be considered gray? And why gray?" Her pace picked up. "Because the *reason* we're taking it isn't for personal pleasure, it's for—" She halted in front of Brian's locker and tapped him on the back. "Brian?"

His surprise turned to wariness. "What?"

"Thank you for funding Harmony House." She wished he looked less forbidding. "Maybe you can come see our kids sometime."

"I'm a killer, remember?" he said, then looked ashamed. "Sorry, that wasn't cool."

"I'm the one who said it," she reminded him ruefully.

"You had a reason." He shoved his hands in his pockets. "Listen, I know how you feel about my father's business and all—"

"But I shouldn't have screamed in your face—"

"Wait, let me finish. It's hard to say and I still can't really believe it." He took a deep breath. "I read those posters you put out and looked at all those pictures and . . . well, on Monday I quit my job. I can't do it now that I know what I'm selling."

For once, Janis was speechless.

"My father's pretty p.o.'d. He says I'm betraying him and if I'm so gung-ho to make my own decisions, then I can pay all my own bills now, too." He gave her a wry smile. "Know anybody who's looking for an unemployed high school kid who works hard?"

"Yeah," she croaked. "Me."

"I was hoping you'd say that," he said, hugging her.

Sixteen

Cassandra perched on the edge of the couch, smiling in case Stephanie looked her way and desperately wishing it was time to leave. The coffee table was heaped with beer cups sporting soggy cigarettes, pizza crusts, chicken bones, and stained napkins. The air was thick with smoke and the blaring metal music pounded her head like a sledgehammer.

I shouldn't have come, she thought. I should have dropped Natalie off and gone back home to practice my solo. I belong in the dance studio, not here. I don't fit in with these people.

"Hey, sweet thing." A guy she didn't recognize plopped down next to her and offered her a hit off his joint.

"No, thanks," she mumbled, embarrassed for him. His eyes were tomato-red and snaked with veins, his movements clumsy, and he had a big hunk of something stuck between his front teeth.

"Don't tell me you're not partying," he said in a loud, slurred voice and squeezed her knee.

She looked at his hand, nostrils flaring. There was food stuck under his fingernails.

"Hey," the guy breathed, sticking his face close to hers and nodding down in the direction of her chest. "You got a fine set of hooters, you know."

Mortified, Cassandra jumped up and strode away.

"Kiss me, Stephie," Phillip said with a big, sloppy grin. He backed her against the fridge and kissed her with a wildness she hadn't felt since they'd first started going out. "C'mon, let's go into my room. Gotta celebrate your birthday, you know."

"I know," she said breathlessly. "But now."

"Why not?" he coaxed, nuzzling her ear. "C'mon, it'll only take a minute."

"Oh, big thrill," she teased, laughing and squirming out of his embrace. Her movements knocked the paper with his parents' St. Kitts hotel number off the fridge and she tacked it back up.

"Later, then," he said, recapturing her. "Stay with me tonight, Steph. Your old lady won't even know you're gone."

She hesitated, tempted. Her mother *would* know she was gone but if she told her she was staying at a friend's house . . . "Okay," she said, smiling up into his bleary eyes.

"Really?" He staggered, clapping a playful hand over his heart. "What made you say yes? The necklace, the sweater, or me?"

"You," she said, kissing him. "Although the

198

necklace and the sweater are a close second." The necklace was a simple, gold chain bearing a diamond chip and the sweater was pink cashmere, a gorgeous replacement for the one he'd spilled coffee on.

"Gold digger," he murmured. "Love you, Steph."

"Love you, too," she said.

"Phil?" Jared said, coming into the kitchen. "C'mon man, the speedball express is gettin' ready to pull out."

"What does he mean?" Stephanie whispered.

"Nothing," Phillip said with a tender, amused smile. "It's an inside joke. Don't worry about it."

But she was worried and tightened her arms around his waist. "Stay with me," she whispered. "Don't go with him."

"I'll be back," he promised, unwinding her arms.

The speedball express, Stephanie repeated silently, watching them head upstairs. Maybe Natalie will know what that means.

Natalie stood in the corner of the living room, pretending to listen to some drunk girl's babble but keeping her gaze on the door. If it opened and Edan walked in, she would see him.

And he would see her.

Come on, she thought, sending him a silent summons.

"Hot, baby."

Maria turned, wobbling slightly and eyed the guy sitting on the dining room table behind her. He had on a biker jacket, a red bandana, and he looked older than the other kids. "You think so?" she said, sauntering into the room. Her beer splashed out over her hand and she licked it off, giggling.

He nodded, watching her and smiling slightly.

"Well, that just goes to show you," she said, planting her cup on the table and a hand on each of his knees. His muscles tensed but he didn't move away. "What would you say if I told you that's what everybody else thinks too, but they're wrong?"

He shrugged. "I'd say prove it."

"Prove what? That I'm not hot? How'm I supposed to do that?"

"Like this," he said and cupping a hand behind her head, pulled her face to his. His mouth was hard, the kiss a demand rather than a request.

Maria closed her eyes, letting the murkiness in her brain wash away the immediate surge of revulsion. She stayed numb until dark, black panic dropped like a curtain. "I can't," she mumbled, twisting her mouth away. "Lemme go."

He did, watching as she stumbled back a few steps.

"See?" she gasped and wheeling, rushed out.

"You guys aren't drinking?" Phillip said, lurching up to Janis and Brian. "C'mon, it's a party, man."

"We're designated drivers," Janis said, staring at

200

him worriedly. His face was so white, his eyes glittered like obsidian, and his entire body was shaking.

"Maria's the only one of all of you who's having any fun."

"Then we'd better drive her home," Janis said to Brian.

"You guys are like old ladies," Phillip said and veered off.

Cassandra locked the bathroom door and stared at the front of her turtleneck. Her breasts looked the same as always, small and firm, a ballerina's breasts, not big enough to make that ninny with the grubby nails follow her around all night. And yet he wouldn't leave her alone.

Are they that noticeable? she fretted, turning sideways. Oh, no, what if they're getting bigger? How am I supposed to dance?

How could her body play such a dirty trick on her?

Maria stood in the dining room doorway, staring at the guy she'd kissed. Her mind, clearer than before but still muzzy with beer, had sent her back for an answer. She stepped into the room.

"Hey, baby," he said, idly swinging his legs.

"So?" He had a moustache—she hadn't noticed that before—and deep, dark eyes. "What did you decide?"

He shrugged. "Too quick to tell."

Maria took another step, then another, drawn to him in a way she didn't understand. He wasn't moving or reaching, he was just sitting there, watching, waiting for her to come to him. "You remind me of someone." She reached out and touched his moustache, running her fingers over the bristly hairs. Her stomach clenched and suddenly she was kissing him, soft and slow and the way she wanted to be kissed, with love and tenderness and caring . . .

He reminded her of Mr. Garcia.

He didn't touch her but let her go on and on, drawing back only when she couldn't contain her tears.

"My loss," he said, pointing her firmly towards the door.

"Natalie?" Cassandra touched her arm. "Time to go."

Natalie tore her gaze from the door and shoulders slumped, followed her cousin over to the couch to get Maria.

I called to him, she thought thickly, and he didn't come.

"What a mess," Stephanie said, staring at the empty, littered living room. It was almost three-thirty, she'd just said goodbye to the last guest, and was nearly asleep on her feet. Jared had crashed on the family room floor and stifling the urge to kick him, she shut the light and went upstairs.

"Phillip?" she called softly, padding into his room. The moonlight fell across the bed, silhouetting his sleeping form; smiling, she perched on the edge of the mattress to slip off her shoes. Looks like we won't need a condom tonight, she thought, patting his arm. Her movements slowed, then went still.

He was so quiet.

"Phillip?" Her voice wavered, breaking the ominous silence. She squeezed his arm, shaking him. "Boy, you're really out of it. Phillip? Wake up. It's me, Stephie."

He didn't move. Didn't snore. Mumble. Roll over.

She leaped up, snatching her hand away and stared at him. "Oh, God," she said, starting to tremble. "Oh, God Phillip, wake up." She stumbled across the room to the light and flicked it on. "Phillip, wake up, please wake up."

Nothing.

"Don't do this," she cried, rushing back to the bed. She grabbed his arm, grunting as she rolled him onto his back and fumbled with the hand that flopped over the edge. "Pulse, pulse, oh, God, I don't even know where to look!" Sobbing, she whipped her hair behind her ear and pressed it to his chest.

Nothing.

"No," she cried, tugging up his t-shirt and trying again. His skin was warm and there . . . there . . . faintly faintly faintly . . .

"Don't stop," she said fiercely, scrambling out of the room on all fours and taking the stairs at a dead run. "Jared! Jared! Help me, something's wrong with Phillip. He's hardly breathing!"

"Huh?" He sat up, dazed.

Stephanie skittered past him into the kitchen and grabbed the phone. Her hand was shaking so badly she couldn't make her fingers punch out the numbers.

"What're you doing?"

"Calling 911," she cried, hanging up and trying again. "Phillip's hardly breathing, Jared. His lips are blue and . . ." She broke off, gaping as he gathered his stuff. "What're you doing?"

"You never saw me tonight," he said, giving her a hard look and bolting out the door.

She stood there, open-mouthed, then stiffened one finger and pressed 911. "My name is Stephanie Ling," she said, bursting into tears when they answered. "Please send an ambulance. I think my boyfriend is dying." She gave them the address, then crept upstairs to stay with Phillip until they got there.

"Hurry," she whispered, laying her head on his chest to listen for his faint heartbeat. "Hurry."

"Where are his parents?" the cop said, jotting Phillip's name and address on his clipboard.

"In St. Kitts," Stephanie said, trying to peer past him into the bedroom. "The phone number's on the fridge. Is he gonna be all right?"

"They're taking good care of him," the cop said. "There was a party here tonight?"

"My b . . . birthday," she said, gulping back tears.

"What did he do? Drink?"

"I think so," she said, frowning as she tried to remember. The room was spinning and the party seemed like it had taken place eons ago. "Oh, how could this happen?"

"Drugs?"

"Yes," she said, gritting her teeth as she remembered Jared's warning. It meant nothing compared to Phillip's life. "I think he snorted coke and there was pot here." She met the cop's gaze. "I don't know if this means anything, but what's a 'speedball?' "

An EMS worker said, "Oh, boy."

"A speedball is an often fatal mix of cocaine and either heroin or morphine," the cop said, steadying her as she swayed. "You okay?"

"Heroin," she said and moaning, slid down the wall to the floor. "Oh, Phillip, how could you?"

The cop took her to the hospital in the back of the patrol car. The EMS crew wheeled Phillip in on a gurney and a flurry of tense, white-coated doctors with tired eyes and grim faces carried him off.

"What happens now?" Stephanie asked bewilderedly.

"Dispatch has located his parents and his mother's trying to get a flight home," the cop said.

"She's authorized the hospital to take whatever life-saving procedures are necessary—"

"He could really die, couldn't he?" Stephanie whispered, pressing her fist to her lips. "Or . . . or worse."

The cop gave her a funny look.

"His . . . his brain," she said, overcome with terror. Brain dead people had never seemed real before but now, here, with these awful smells and echoing, low-pitched moans and dry, stifling heat, it seemed all too possible.

"Sit down," the cop said, steering her to one of the hard, plastic chairs and pressing on her shoulders till she sat. "What's your home number? I think it's time to call someone for you."

She whispered the number but the only person she wanted to call was behind those doors and there was no way to reach him.

Seventeen

Stephanie stared down at her hands. Her mother's humiliation hit her like a series of sharp slaps. Drugs. Drinking. Sleeping at her boy friend's. The hospital. The police.

"Your daughter's fine, Mrs. Ling," the cop said, shooting Stephanie a concerned glance. "Apparently, she wasn't doing much besides baby-sitting Phillip tonight and the bottom line is that if she hadn't been there, he wouldn't be here now."

"Thank you," her mother said stiffly. "Stephanie, let's go."

Her head snapped up. "I can't leave him here alone. What if something happens?"

"There is nothing more you can do," Mrs. Ling said.

"I can be here in case he wakes up," Stephanie said.

"Then you'll have to stay alone," her mother said.

She shouldn't have been surprised or hurt but she was.

"Well, I can't leave Anastasia and Corinne home alone all night," her mother said defensively, flushing and turning to the expressionless cop. "Can you bring her home when she's ready?"

"I can't guarantee anything," he said, shrugging. "Depends on the rest of the calls tonight."

Mrs. Ling's lips thinned. Snapping open her purse, she handed Stephanie several crumpled dollars. "Call when you're ready to leave. If I can't come, this is bus fare." She stared at Stephanie for a moment as if to say, 'Thank you' for shaming me and walked stiffly away.

"I'll run you home before my shift ends," the cop said.

"Thanks," Stephanie mumbled, bowing her head.

"Want a cup of coffee?"

"Please." She held out her money but he waved it away.

"Consider it the kindness of strangers," he said.

"Stephanie!"

Stephanie blinked, rubbing her eyes. There was no sign of the cop but a tall, grim-faced woman wearing turquoise stood over her like an avenging angel. "Mrs. Fairweather?"

"What happened?"

"I'm not sure," Stephanie said in a small voice. She had never felt comfortable around Phillip's mother. "How's Phillip?"

"Stabilized," Mrs. Fairweather said shortly. "He's

still in Intensive Care, though and hasn't woken up yet."

He was stable. He was alive. Stephanie started to cry and was surprised when Mrs. Fairweather sank down next to her.

"Stephanie, please tell me what happened," she said wearily.

Hiccuping, Stephanie gave her the most important details.

"Phillip doing heroin?" Mrs. Fairweather said in disbelief. "No. Recreational drugs maybe, but I've never seen—"

"You're never here," she said desperately. "I'm the only one Phillip has, Mrs. Fairweather. You might not agree but that's how he feels. No one's ever home for him. If his friends aren't around, he's alone." She was crying again. "Your career might mean a lot to you but all he knows is that you care more about chasing celebrity gossip than you do about him."

"That's not true," Mrs. Fairweather said, going pale. "He's my child; I would do anything for him."

"Then stick around," Stephanie cried. "I mean, would it be that hard to take an assignment closer to home?"

Mrs. Fairweather stared at her. "It's not that easy."

"So you'll do anything . . . but that." She looked away. "I guess I'll go home now." She spotted the waiting cop and rose. "I'll find a way back later to see him."

"Stephanie." Mrs. Fairweather avoided her eyes.

"I phoned some of the best doctors in the country on the way here and they all agree he needs professional help, so I've signed him into a de-tox center up north."

Stephanie couldn't breathe. "What? When? For how long?"

"As soon as he can be transported. And until he's well."

Stephanie's knees buckled.

"You're scheduled to dance at 11:30," Miss Tatiana said, licking a finger and smoothing a wisp of Cassandra's hair back into place. "Third in your category. That's not bad. The judges will still be fresh." Frowning, she tugged at the top of the tutu's satin bodice. "Are you growing?"

"I don't know," Cassandra said, staring helplessly at her chest. "I didn't think so . . ."

"Well, there's nothing we can do about it now," Miss Tatiana said, sighing. "Just try not to bounce." She stepped back, fluffing the drifting, white net. "Everything all right?"

Cassandra bit her lip, haunted by the memory of finding cookies scattered around her driveway this morning. Frantic, she had thrown her dancebag into the BMW, gathered the cookies and heaved them into the street. They're gone now and it's over, she told herself. Concentrate on the competition, Cassandra. Her hands were damp, her stomach tight. "I'm going to the bathroom."

"Be careful," Miss Tatiana said.

The ladies room was crowded with dancers in various stages of undress and Cassandra had to wait for a stall. One short week ago she would have used the time to assess her competition but now all she did was worry. Her parents would be in the audience and while they weren't still mad at her, she could sense their disappointment. Their faith in her had been shaken and only a first place win could restore it.

But she hadn't been practicing.

I shouldn't have spent all that time away from the studio, she thought, rubbing her bare arms. I should have stayed home last night and I shouldn't even have gone to that demonstration. I haven't been focusing and now I'm here, scared to death, unprepared and totally out of control—

"Stall's open," said the girl behind her. "You're next."

"Thanks." She hurried in and shut the door. Her heart was pounding and her stomach clenched like a fist. I have to relax, she thought, struggling with her costume. I have to get a grip.

Harsh retching echoed out of the next stall.

Cassandra stiffened. "Are you okay?"

"Yeah," someone gasped. "No sweat. I always throw up beforehand." A chuckle. "It makes me dance better."

"Nerves," Cassandra said.

"No, I do it on purpose," the girl said, gagging again. "Eat to satisfy the hunger, barf it up to satisfy the body." The toilet flushed and the stall door opened. "Now I'm ready."

Curious, Cassandra exited also. The girl was at the sink, dressed in a dreamy pink tutu. She was slender, ethereal, with a swanlike neck, no chest, and a body far too fragile for something as violent as vomiting. "Are you sure you're all right?"

The girl laughed and patted her hollow stomach. "Ask me when I've won that trophy." Her gaze dropped to Cassandra's abdomen.

Quickly, Cassandra sucked it in.

The girl laughed again and flitted away.

Natalie stood in the kitchen, listening to her aunt and uncle getting ready upstairs.

I have maybe five minutes till we leave for the competition, she thought, staring at the phone. Should I?

"Ready, Natalie?" Aunt Miriam's voice wafted downstairs.

"Yeah." She cleared her throat and before she could talk herself out of it, snatched the receiver and punched out the Poppy Street number she'd committed to memory.

"Hello?" A feminine voice, young and smooth.

Natalie said nothing.

"Hello?"

"Hi," she said finally. Her face was burning. She should have hung up. "Is . . . um, Edan there?"

"No, I think he's out with Jesse. Who's this?"

A fool, Natalie thought, starting to hang up. She hesitated, listening as the girl said, "Want to leave a message?"

212

"Uh . . . yeah." She stumbled over the words. "Just tell him . . . um, Natalie called, okay, and I'll call back."

"Okay," the girl said. "Bye."

"Wait," Natalie blurted, gripping the receiver. "Um . . . who are you? I mean, who am I talking to?"

"Oh, I'm Cleo," the girl said cheerfully. "Bye now."

Natalie stared at the dead receiver. *Cleo?*

Cassandra stood on the sidelines, watching as the girl in the pink tutu floated around the dance floor like a butterfly.

"She's your only real competition," Miss Tatiana murmured, rubbing Cassandra's frigid fingers between her own. "She has a perfect form but not as much experience as you, Cassandra. And her music is dull."

But her dancing isn't, Cassandra thought miserably. She looks weightless, while here I am with my bouncing 'hooters.'

The ballerina finished and the applause was deafening.

"Next on point, Cassandra Taylor representing Miss Tatiana's School of Dance," the MC said when the judges had finished writing. "She will be performing to 'Wuthering Heights.' "

"Remember the passion," Miss Tatiana whispered. "Go."

Cassandra moved dazedly to the center of the

213

floor and took her position. She heard the music but it washed over her, leaving her stranded like a shell on the beach. She danced on, desperate to recapture the magic but it eluded her, making her feel awkward and contrived, making a mockery of the song's heartache.

Face flaming, Cassandra whirled in a series of pirouettes, barely registering the audience's hushed, admiring stir. She was dying, she was a bad joke gone public. She hadn't practiced and the control she'd lost was a sick, sour lump in her stomach.

The song ended. The audience clapped.

Cassandra looked at Miss Tatiana.

They both knew the truth.

"Thank you," Stephanie said, paying the taxi driver and running into the Emergency Room. "I'm here to see Phillip Fairweather," she said, gripping the counter. "He was brought in this morning."

The desk nurse consulted her computer terminal. "I'm sorry hon, he's being readied for transfer."

Stephanie blanched. *"Already?* But he just got here!"

"Apparently he's in good enough condition to be moved."

"Please can I see him?" Stephanie said, near tears. "I have to see him before he goes. I don't have a car, I don't even know where they're taking him, please . . ."

The nurse gave her a thoughtful look. "Are you the girl who was with him when he overdosed?"

"Yes. Oh, please, I promise I won't upset him—"

214

"Five minutes. Third curtain on the right." The nurse smiled. "And if anybody asks, you're his sister."

"Thank you." Stephanie hurried into Intensive Care.

"Congratulations," Natalie cried, giving Cassandra an enthusiastic bear hug. "You were so good!"

"Thanks," Cassandra said, watching her parents.

"Very nice," her father said, kissing her cheek. "With a little more hard work, next time it'll be First Place."

Cassandra's throat squeezed shut. She looked pleadingly at her mother, offering up her Third Place medal.

"It's nice that they give out prizes to those other than the winner," her mother said, examining it. "I guess it's a way of making everyone feel included. Lovely, dear. That'll look nice on the bulletin board in your room."

But not on the mantelpiece in the den, Cassandra thought miserably. That honor was reserved for the winners in the family.

The girl in the pink tutu drifted by, cradling the First Place trophy and wearing a triumphant smile.

"God, she's skinny," Natalie said, watching her pass. "She looks like a Q-Tip."

She looks perfect, Cassandra thought.

"Well, come on," Mr. Taylor rumbled, checking his watch. "I reserved a table at Pierre's to celebrate Cassandra's victory but I guess we can still use it." He laughed and herded them out.

The restaurant was elegant. Cassandra ate a four course meal and, when she got home, went straight into the bathroom.

She stared at the toilet for a moment, then knelt and stuck her finger down her throat.

Oh, Phillip, Stephanie cried silently, staring at his sleeping face. He looked different here, small and vulnerable, surrounded by tubes and monitors and sheets so white they hurt her eyes. He wasn't hers anymore and she was afraid to touch him, afraid a bell would go off or a monitor would sound its alarm.

"Steph." His voice was scarcely a whisper.

"Hi," she said, clenching her teeth so she wouldn't start bawling. "How do you feel?"

"Like crap." He tried to lift his head and couldn't. "Come close, Stephie. I need to touch you."

Now her tears fell freely, splashing the limp hand she held to her cheek. "I was so scared for you."

"C'mere," he murmured, drawing her face down to his chest and stroking her hair. "My mom's here, Steph. She's taking me to a rehab joint up in Bellingham."

So far away, Stephanie thought, heart sinking.

"It's weird," he whispered. "I'm almost glad, you know? I mean, she really looked worried. She *cried*."

The wonder in his voice broke her heart.

"Will you call me if you can?" she said, kissing

his hand.

"Hey," he laughed weakly. "I'll send you post-cards."

The curtain was shoved aside. "We're ready to go."

Stephanie met the doctor's gaze. "One second," she said, wiping her eyes on her sleeve. "Be good and get well," she said, staring at his dear, familiar face. She wanted to cling to him, to hold him here with her and never let him go. "Come home soon."

"I'll try." His eyelids drooped. " 'Night, Steph."

"Bye, Phillip. I love you."

"Me, too," he mumbled, sighing.

Eighteen

The hallway was still, the lockers bearing silent witness as Maria waited outside Mr. Garcia's classroom. If the door hadn't been locked she would have waited inside, at his desk, in his chair.

The clock on the wall said 7:15.

She tensed as *shushing* footsteps came towards her.

"Well, good morning," Mr. Garcia said surprisedly, rounding the corner. He was carrying his briefcase and a cup of coffee. "What're you doing here so early?"

"Waiting for you."

"Lucky me," he said and smiling, fumbled for his keys.

"I'll hold that for you," she said, putting her hand over his and easing the steaming coffee from his grasp.

"Thanks," he said, missing the softness in her gaze.

The door swung open and he reached past her to

flick on the lights. She breathed deep, pulling his scent into her body.

"After you," he said, waving her forward.

"Thank you." She set the coffee on his desk and watched him get situated. His easy, unhurried motions soothed her, the hushed room created a sense of intimacy she'd only dreamed about.

"If I had known you were coming, I would've baked a cake," he teased, smothering a yawn. "Sorry, I'm no good without caffeine."

"Yes, you are," she said, held by his warm gaze and the way his eyes met hers directly, not detouring first to her chest, as if the best part of her lay under a sweater. He treated her with respect, like she was someone whose thoughts and feelings mattered.

"You're being very mysterious this morning, Maria," he said, smiling and sipping his coffee. "Ah, that's better. Now, what can I do for you?" He leaned back in his chair and ran a hand over his thinning hair, watching her curiously. "Is anything wrong?"

"No, I just wanted to tell you something." Her knees were shaking. She had so much to lose. "I went to a party Saturday night and met a biker who had a mustache just like yours."

"It needed a trim?" Mr. Garcia said, his smile fading as he caught her agonized expression. "Sorry. Go ahead."

Go ahead. So simple and yet so hard. "I kissed him." She was barely breathing. "I . . . I pretended he was you."

Mr. Garcia went still.

"It was beautiful," she continued, lost in the fantasy. "You were sweet and caring and you didn't try to get anything off of me, you didn't grab me or curse me or call me a tease . . ." Her voice broke and her eyes filled with tears. "You didn't hurt me and I j . . . just wanted t . . .to tell you I l . . . love you for that."

"Who hurt you, Maria?" he asked quietly, placing his hand over hers. "Tell me, please."

She closed her eyes, reeling, and whispered, "Leif."

Nineteen

"Hey Steph?" Corinne tugged gently on Stephanie's blankets. "It's time to get up for school."

Stephanie rolled over. "I'm not going to school today."

Corinne's jaw dropped. "What? Stephie, are you sick?"

"No," she said, opening her eyes and staring dully at the ceiling. "I'm scared."

"Oh." Silence. "Because of Phillip?"

She nodded, keeping her gaze on the cracked plaster. If it fell and crushed her, she couldn't hurt anymore than she already did. "I miss him. I'm scared at what it'll be like without him."

Corinne patted Stephanie's head. "He'll be back."

Will he? she wondered, clinging to her little sister's hand. Oh, I hope so.

Janis sat in the Bronco, battling a skein of fuzzy, neon green yarn. "C'mon," she muttered, yanking at a snarl.

Brian opened the passenger door and climbed in. "Hi," he said, giving her a quick kiss. "What the heck are you doing?"

"I'm *trying* to crotchet booties for our kids," she said grimly, holding up a lumpy, misshapen circle. "The Yarn Shoppe donated the yarn, the hook, and the instruction manual."

"They should've donated an instructor, too," he said, lips twitching. "That sucker looks like a moldy, mutant lime."

"Really?" Eyes gleaming, she handed him the mass. "Well then, why don't *you* show me the correct way to crotchet?"

"Oh, no," he said, laughing and dumping it back in her lap. "I'd do an awful lot for you Janis, but there's just no way . . ."

"We'll see," she said with a small, smug smile.

"Maria, how did he hurt you?" Mr. Garcia asked softly.

Her breath hitched. "I c . . . can't tell you."

"Why not? We're friends, aren't we?"

"You won't want to be when you find out about me," she mumbled, hanging her head. "I'm . . ." She couldn't even say it.

"Maybe you should talk to a woman counselor—"

"No!" She swallowed hard. "Promise you won't hate me, Mr. Garcia? Promise you won't think I'm a disgusting person?"

"That's the easiest promise in the world," he said.

She met his gaze and began to talk.

"Well, I don't agree," Natalie said, holding the front door open for Cassandra. "I consider Third Place pretty good for—"

"Oh my God!" Cassandra cried, dropping her books.

Natalie followed her gaze.

The BMW was littered with cookies.

And someone had slashed the 'n' word along the door in soap.

Cassandra ran to her car and with one wild motion, swept the cookies to the ground. "No more, do you hear me, Natalie? Don't bait them, don't antagonize them, don't even *see* them! They're dangerous, they came into our *driveway* to do this! What's gonna be next, our house? No! No more!"

Natalie took her arm and steered her away from the car. "Saying 'no more' isn't gonna change anything. See that filth on your car door? That makes this a hate crime." Her eyes darkened. "It's time to call the cops."

"No," Cassandra moaned. "If we make a big deal, they're only going to harass us more. Let's just let it die now. Please?"

"Cass," Natalie said sadly. "Don't you get it? This isn't the end, this is only the beginning."

Look for Girlfriends #3: *Deal Me Out*—in your bookstore right now!